Without Limits

DUSTIN GRINNELL

For more information, please contact Dustin Grinnell at: www.dustingrinnell.com.
Cover design: Bob Zaccardi (Kindle) and Mark Bushy (print)

ISBN: 0692376364
ISBN 13: 9780692376362

"My good blade carves the casques of men,
My tough lance thrusteth sure,
My strength is as the strength of ten,
Because my heart is pure."

"Sir Galahad" by Alfred Lord Tennyson

THESSALONIKI
PAROS

KITROS
SALT PIT

DION

MT OLYMPUS

PARAMYTHIA

N
W · E
S

AEGEAN
SEA

DELPHI

SPIROS LOUIS
OLYMPIC
STADIUM

EGALEO
MOUNTAIN
THE
ACROPOLIS

IONIAN SEA

SPARTA

SWIM 12 MILES (19 K.M.) ———
BIKE 560 MILES (900 K.M.) ———
RUN 131 MILES (211 K.M.) ———

THE ALETHEIA
QUINTUPLE ULTRA-TRIATHLON

Introduction

The word *philosophy* comes from the Ancient Greek word *philosophia,* meaning 'the love of wisdom.' We tend to think of philosophy as abstract, disconnected from modern-day problems. Socrates, the father of modern philosophy, is often pictured as a wild, white-haired old man, mumbling in public spaces, nitpicking at the order of things. But Plato showed that Socrates only urged people to question the 'truths' they held on to so tightly. He urged people to see situations and people as well as their own thoughts and actions as they truly are, and to then behave authentically. Fundamentally, philosophy is the search for truth, but as Socrates and many other philosophers have found, this noble pursuit can come at profound personal costs.

Socrates dealt with perhaps the most practical questions humans could ask: How should we live our lives? Where should we focus our efforts? How should we conduct ourselves? Such answers don't reveal themselves easily. Perhaps this is why rigorous philosophical inquiry often leads to doubt, anxiety, and uncertainty. However, most who engage in such thinking would likely agree that it's better to suffer these mental disturbances over self-delusion.

What is the purpose of philosophy, though? One answer may be that it is to see oneself and the world with greater clarity, to rid oneself of pride and self-deception in order to achieve peace of mind. According to Socrates, such an "examined life" produces the highest virtue. Socrates' most gifted pupil was Plato, and Plato's student was Aristotle. To Aristotle, the purpose of life was to achieve *eudaemonia*, or well-being, which is another way of saying *happiness.*

Mostly, philosophy deals in "shoulds." Should we act in our own self-interest, or work for the needs of the collective? Should we focus on the fruits of our labors, or value the process alone? Far from absolutes, such questions allow us to explore complex issues from many angles, to root out larger meanings, and to acknowledge that we may be blind to an unseen whole. As Plato suggested in the introduction to *The Republic*, "Wisdom begins when a man finds out that he does not know what he thinks he knows."

In sports, perhaps the biggest "should" is whether or not to play by the rules. But rather than focus on the rules, perhaps we should examine the individual behind the choice to play fair. The question then becomes how should we *conduct* ourselves, rather than what is the "right" thing to do. According to Aristotle's ethical philosophy, this is the cultivation of character.

Broadly speaking, *eudaemonia* can be interpreted to mean enjoying a good, fortunate life. In Ancient Greece, cultivation of this ideal could be achieved by following the four cardinal virtues of courage, justice, temperance, and prudence. Possessing all four virtues equipped one with the "unity of virtues," an ultimate goodness termed magnanimity, which is Latin for great-souled. Life's ultimate purpose, according to Aristotle, was to become a *megalopsychos*, that is to say a great-souled man.

The path to acquiring such virtue is the accumulation of wisdom through practice. Such wisdom is hard-won, but equips one with the knowledge and sensitivity to behave appropriately in many situations, including sports. Encouraging athletes to follow the rules, to play fair, to do the right thing will not take additional rules or the strict adherence to new principles, but rather a shift in consciousness, triggered by an agent of good—a great-souled man, perhaps—who, through accumulated wisdom, shows the world that virtue is not what you do, but what you are.

Prologue

Tianjiin province, Northern China

It was the Great Wall Marathon, and one runner was far ahead of the rest, freakishly fast. The others trailed behind, the challenges of the route too much, but the leader kept pushing forward. Michael McKnight didn't think of himself as a cheat. He was what his father needed him to be: a brave test subject in a profound experiment that just might revolutionize endurance sports forever. And maybe get him that win he had always wanted, too.

Most of the Great Wall was in ruins, the challenging route covered in loose stone, gravel, and missing steps. Michael barely noticed as he sprinted past panoramic views of lush forests and mountain peaks looming beyond quiet green hills blanketed in mist. He followed a turn around a decaying watchtower, one of many massive defensive structures built to ward off invasions from barbarians outside the Celestial Empire.

From a distant courtyard, two men watched Michael skip up the granite steps, now almost an hour ahead of the East African runners in second and third place, according to the official times.

"Are you recording this?" Michael's father asked. Jack McKnight was a clean-cut man with chiseled features, a trim body for 52 years old, and brown hair with some grays swirling through like a hint of dark cloud. His hazel-colored eyes were concealed by the binoculars pressed to his face, but they were always lively, almost luminous. McKnight was dressed in a black Valentino suit made by appointment-only in New York City, conveniently in the same building on Park Avenue as the McKnight Charitable Trust, the fourth wealthiest philanthropic trust in the United States.

McKnight leaned toward the scientist who had helped develop the artificial red blood cells pumping through the runner's muscles, feeding his brain with rich oxygen. "Well done, Dr. Weng."

The scientist, Dr. Kevin Weng, said nothing for a second or two, nor did he take his eyes away from the video camera. He had only perfected the technology three days previously, though. He deserved a moment or two to admire it.

"When do I tell this Ms. Brines I've solved her challenge?" Weng asked eventually. Of course that would be his main concern.

"We will call DARPA after the race." McKnight had registered his son for the May marathon on a whim. It had been too perfect an opportunity to ignore. He had asked him to test the respirocytes and Michael had jumped at the chance, even though he had been banned from marathons in the United States. A marathon on the Great Wall of China seemed the perfect testing ground for the ingenious drug. With its 5,164 steps and steep ascents along the Simatai and Jinshanling sections of the historic structure, the marathon was far more difficult than most.

"What exactly is the drug?" Michael had asked the night before the race in the luxurious room in a five-star hotel he had been staying in thanks to his father.

"Think of it as next-generation doping," McKnight had said over a hot bowl of noodles. "No chance of being caught, and far greater effects. The details of the respirocytes… well, are you really interested, or do you just want to win?"

Michael had shrugged. McKnight smiled as Weng plunged the syringe into his son's arm to inject the nanotechnology-based drug. The project had originally been put forward to the world as an outsourcing project by Dana Brines, the Director of the Defense Advanced Research Projects Agency (DARPA), a research organization that developed advanced technologies for the US military. Weng had solved it. McKnight had made the most of it.

As the route along the Wall steepened, the climb became more strenuous, but Michael had little trouble and hopped up a series of marble steps with boundless energy. He let out a deep, phlegmy cough that stopped him for a moment. He continued, shaking his head.

"See him coughing?" Weng asked. "It's a bad sign. You should consider pulling him from the race, Mr. McKnight."

McKnight considered it. It was his son, after all. It didn't take long for him to make up his mind. "He doesn't have long until the finish."

While other athletes looked tormented by the run, bent over and gripping the crumbling wall for breaks, Michael's lungs were full, his muscles inexhaustible. With two miles left, he was on pace to destroy the Great Wall's marathon record, a time of 3 hours and 10 minutes. The stares from spectators spurred him on in spite of the cough, dumbfounded as he ran passed them at a mind-bending pace.

"We'll meet him at the finish," McKnight said, still peering through his binoculars. "Have re-sus gear ready."

The two men entered their van, making their way to the finish. They sped across mangled dirt roads, passing mangrove trees and men and woman on porches or gardens. The road was paved, but cracked in places, some parts nearly impassable. From tiny stones to shattered boulders, remnants of the broken Wall were everywhere. They crossed a series of small bridges and passed through villages with single-storied farm houses with roofs of Chinese tile. They reached the base of the Wall where the finish line was, and climbed a brick pathway to where they would greet their test subject.

Nearly five minutes from the finish, Michael's cough had worsened and he was sweating more than he had all race. His skin was pale as well. But this did little to dampen his spirits. He knew this would be his big moment. He would finally have the glory for which he had always hoped. He daydreamed his way through the discomfort, thinking of what they would all eat to celebrate. Maybe a fresh plate of beans, greens, tomatoes, and eggs from the gardens littering the route, with a delicious Tsingtao beer to wash it all down.

As the finish line came into view, Michael took one last glance at the stunning hillsides, the mountains with ancient towers on top. For the first time in the race, he took a second to appreciate it. Before, it had been an irrelevance. The finishing time was the only thing that mattered. He could just make out farmers working in fields in the distance.

A series of coughs doubled him over, slowing his pace again. Streaks of bright-red blood showed on the back of his hand when he brought it away, but he'd come so far now. Too far to even consider stopping. Michael pushed on the last few strides, down the finishing straight.

When he splashed through the plastic tape across the finish line, the spectators greeted him with awe. Michael had finished the marathon in two hours and three minutes, a great time for most other races, and an impossible time on the Great Wall of China.

As the coughing worsened, Michael tried to ignore it. This was his moment. The realization of his fantasy. Yet with so many reporters and bewildered race volunteers around him, it was impossible to focus on the victory. His cough produced more blood, which Michael smeared away with the back of his hand. He pushed through the crowd, no longer triumphant, but fearful. He saw his father, heading towards him with Dr. Weng.

"Guess the respirocytes work," McKnight said. He puffed a cigar to life with a lighter.

"How do you feel?" Weng asked.

Michael coughed and held his stomach. "Bad cough," he said, cringing, "but I'm alright, I guess. This stuff is like nothing I've ever tried. I just ran flat out, never once winded. How do these things work?"

"Let's get you back to the van," McKnight said, eyeing a reporter jogging their way. "We'll talk about it there. Take care of things."

The reporter was a heavy-set Chinese man with a square face and horn-rimmed glasses. He pulled a hand-held video camera from his pocket. "Sir... sir...can you explain how you just did that?"

Michael coughed and then spit a pink glob on the ground. He stepped toward the reporter, knowing that he should take his spotlight. But McKnight darted in between the two.

"No questions," he said, blowing smoke in the reporter's face.

The reporter waved the smoke away. "What are you, his dad?"

"Yes, as it happens. And his sponsor. Which is the same thing in this business."

Weng grabbed Michael underneath his armpits and helped him down the steep pathway. McKnight followed, leaving the reporter without his quotes. The reporter yelled after them, but didn't follow.

"People are going to want to know how this happened. No way did you do this clean!"

That was as far as it went though. One of the advantages of China: people in the media knew better than to ask the wrong questions too loudly.

Michael fell to his knees and vomited. "I don't know what's wrong with me." His voice was shaky. He looked at the mess on the ground, a pool of bright-red blood.

"Get him up," McKnight said, smoke billowing from his cigar.

Weng lifted Michael, and dragged him to the end of the pathway.

"You're feeling the side effects right now," McKnight said.

The young man's face contorted. "Side effects?" He coughed deeply. "You didn't say anything about *side effects*."

McKnight looked at the scientist. "We didn't know for certain that there would be any. That's why we test these things. Doctor…"

Weng looked sympathetic, as he delivered the reality. "The pressure within the capillaries in your lungs has increased to a point where fluid has begun to leak back into the air sacs where gas transfer happens."

Michael looked horrified. His face was ashen.

Weng helped him lumber into the van. "Are you finding it difficult to breathe?"

Michael dropped to his knees. Staring at the van's floor, he managed to nod his head. "There must… be something… you can do…"

It was an effort even to get the words out.

"Maybe if we'd gotten to you sooner," Dr. Weng said. He looked over at McKnight.

"We wouldn't have had proof then," McKnight said. "And my son wouldn't have had his victory. It's worth it, Michael. You understand that, don't you? It's *worth* it."

Michael couldn't even catch his breath enough to argue. Dr. Weng put a hand on his shoulder.

"Your lungs are filling with fluid. It's called pulmonary edema, and it's affecting the exchange of gas into your blood. Soon, your body will not be able to get oxygen and you will become hypoxic."

"It feels like I'm–"

"Drowning, yes." Weng lowered his head. "I'm sorry."

McKnight put a hand on his son's back. "The first one through the wall always gets bloodied. But you did it, Michael."

Michael slapped his father's hand away and then jerked upward, hitting his head on the van's ceiling. His cough had a disturbing crackling sound, as if he was gurgling water.

Weng turned to McKnight. "The crackling sound is called 'rales.' It's the last step."

Michael spit a glob of blood onto the floor and then lunged toward McKnight. But he didn't have the strength. McKnight stepped away and Michael tumbled to the floor helplessly. He wheezed, closed his eyes, and then laid down on his back.

McKnight knelt beside him. "You made history here today, son."

Michael's chest bounced up and down rapidly as he searched for air. He gasped and then let out another vicious cough, ejecting blood on his lips. Some dribbled down his chin. "Why are you doing this?"

McKnight let out a heavy sigh. "Your birth was an accident, you know. I never told you that. Your mother didn't want you, but I did."

Michael forced his next words out. "She might have left, but she wanted me more than you ever did."

McKnight laid a hand gently on his son's damp hair. "You don't have to think about this anymore."

Michael looked at the gold bracelet around McKnight's wrist. Etched in the metal was a well-proportioned figure holding a leaf-shaped spear and shield. The figure wore body armor, a robe, and an open-faced helmet.

"Achilles pursued a life of greatness," McKnight said. "Of glory. You will die a hero like he did."

Michael stared up, unable to reply. He gasped, and then there was nothing. His eyes locked in place and his body went limp.

McKnight placed two fingers on Michael's jugular, confirming his son's death. The price of his victory. He stepped into the van's driver's seat and reached into his pocket. He pulled out a syringe full of respirocytes suspended in a clear liquid. He rolled the window down, rested his arm on the door, and restarted his cigar. He took a long draw and blew smoke out the window. "A year from now, the *Aletheia* will take place in Greece."

He didn't know if he was talking to Weng, his dead son, or the world as a whole.

McKnight looked regal in the fading light. "According to Greek mythology, Prometheus stole fire and gave it to humanity. For that theft, he was punished by Zeus, and sentenced to eternal torment. Do you know *why* he was punished, Dr. Weng?" He didn't wait for him to answer. "Because the gods believed that mortals couldn't handle fire. They thought it was beyond our capacity." He lifted the syringe into the sunlight. "The gods underestimated man. There are no limits to man's capacity. And next year I will prove that."

He tossed his cigar out the window. "Now let's get you to DARPA."

Part I

"Who has gone farthest? For I would go farther.
And who has been bold and true?
For I would be the boldest and truest being of the universe."

— WALT WHITMAN

One

One year later
Somewhere over the Atlantic

Dana Brines had wanted to sleep on the flight to Athens, but her mind was too busy for that to happen. She glanced at McKnight snoring in the window seat beside her. She loved sitting near the window, but McKnight had taken it automatically. It was his jet, after all.

She kept her eyes open. Every time she closed her eyes, it brought with it the image of thousands of athletes, all dropping to their knees to bleed out on the Olympic fields. It wasn't a reality, not yet, but it would be. It had to be. The opening ceremony would be unforgettable.

Spectators would cheer and stomp, shaking the magnificent stadium in Athens. There would be music, fireworks, dancing. It would be a glorious ode to Greece's mythological beginnings. But Dana's contribution would be more profound. In the midst of the celebration and symbolism, she would destroy those athletes who had chosen to throw aside that Olympic ideal. The ones who had decided to supplement with the performance-enhancing technology she had helped create at DARPA would die.

Justice would be done, no matter how terrible it was.

Her original plan had been to kill her son's murderer. To take a gun or a knife and just put an end to Jack McKnight. That had been grief talking though, and there had been no poetry to it. It had seemed obvious that he should suffer what he had made Michael suffer. That meant using the respirocytes he brought to her. The ones he expected her to make safe, as though it didn't matter that he'd just spent their son's life like it was nothing.

At first, the plan had been simply to inject him with them, but after a year of being hounded by insatiable athletes and coaches, it had mutated into something else. Because it wasn't enough to just kill Jack McKnight. She needed to find a way to *change* things. That would be real justice.

A cruel justice though. What she was planning now was mass murder. Dana had no illusions about that. But what other way was there? Jack had killed her son to supply those who wanted to win at any cost. Dana couldn't kill him only for everything he had created to keep going like a virus. She needed to stop the whole system, and the only way to change the dopers was to send a simple message: cheat and you die. Who would dare to touch performance enhancement when they never knew which batch would kill them?

McKnight's work would be undone. He could see that before he died.

Dana would have to disappear forever, of course. But with what she took from McKnight's limitless resources, that wouldn't be difficult. The financier owned several islands, some of which had avoided maps. Maybe she would meet a man on the island with firm abs and kind eyes. She would slow her life down and forget about military technology and million-dollar budgets. She wouldn't have to project that high-powered executive facade she'd managed to perfect over the years. She would live… for once. Maybe this island man would want to marry. Maybe they would have a child. And maybe she would raise it, the way she hadn't with Michael.

Dana was shocked that Evan had agreed to fly on McKnight's plane after what they had done to him. *He must love punishment,* she thought. She turned in her seat to see if she could spot him in the back of the plane. He was chatting with the Spanish athlete, Isabella. She was a hot little thing, and had been giving Evan flirty glances since Dana was introduced to the athletes participating in the *Aletheia*. She saw Isabella giggle and pull her hair to the side playfully as Evan delivered the same jokes and grins he'd once given her. Dana was surprised to feel a tinge of jealously. It'd been over a year since she had fired Evan from DARPA, leaving the scientist to his triathlon training. She hadn't expected to feel anything seeing him at the start of the race. But this version of the young man looked strong, pure. What happened to that weakling, wounded from his college soccer days? This new man looked different, like he stood for something. He looked more like her type, a wolf. She respected him for that.

She watched Evan whisper something to Isabella and step into the aisle. As he made his way to the bathroom, Dana slipped out of her seat and bumped into him—accidently on purpose.

* * *

Evan Galloway was no fool. He had seen his old "girlfriend" coming. It was impossible not to when Dana was so beautiful, dark-haired and dark-eyed, toned, and confident. He had seen her glaring at him chat while he flirted with Isabella, whom he had grown quite fond of in the days before the ultra-triathlon. Isabella's green eyes and wavy brown hair were alluring, and she was nothing like the cast iron bitch that Dana was. Evan wasn't afraid of his old boss anymore. Evan had found peace in his trainer's home and the tools to maintain it. He took a deep breath, and let his stomach expand as he inhaled. He had such fond memories of Lucian, his home on the olive grove in Virginia, blissful swims in Black Pond, and bike rides through Mather Gorge.

In a year of training with Lucian Atticus, Evan had had plenty of time to think about what he'd say to Dana when he saw her again. When she bumped into him, he opened his mouth to say all the things he'd rehearsed on hundred-mile training runs, but his mind was betraying him. Why was he blocked? Was he nervous about the triathlon? The race distances were mind-boggling, and he was certainly the underdog. But he knew that wasn't inhibiting him. The truth was worse. He couldn't say what he wanted to say, because he was still that same man Dana had cheated on and then fired a year before.

Even after a year of training his body and mind, after Lucian's inspiring messages, all those old feelings that he thought he'd banished came rushing back. Dana still had a grip on him; he was still at the mercy of the powers that be; the whims of the big machine. He hated himself for that.

Objectively, he knew he wouldn't have a chance in the *Aletheia*. It was five times the distance of an ironman triathlon. Too much for anyone not supplementing to succeed in. McKnight or Evan's brother Luke would win, because the respirocytes made anything else impossible. They were willing to do what it took. How could he keep up with those supplementing with the drug he had helped create? Did anyone really "play fair" anymore? Yet if he went down that road, he would have to manage the shame, like he had done unsuccessfully in college. He was done with that.

Lucian had said that he should think of himself as constantly changing. Like a sculptor, he should chisel away at himself to reveal an ideal vision. What *was* his vision, though? Mostly, he just wanted to feel empowered, to feel that he was living on his own terms, and in control of his own destiny. And maybe, just maybe, David could beat Goliath.

* * *

Dana couldn't hide her disappointment. She had been wrong about the "new" Evan. She recognized all the old signals of weakness in Evan's eyes. As he moved toward the bathroom door to escape, she watched the gears spin in his brain, the same machinery that produced his intellectual restlessness—but which also came with a dark side of self-doubt, uncertainty, and anxiety. Sure, his body was stronger and better conditioned after a year of training, but he was still the sheep he had been. Why had he entered the race? What did he think he was going to achieve?

"You look good," Dana said, willing to try for pleasantness, at least.

"Leave me alone." Evan tried to slip into the plane's bathroom door, but Dana grabbed his shoulder.

"You and that Isabella girl look pretty friendly."

"Not as friendly as you and McKnight."

She looked over at the sleeping man with a disgusted look.

"I figured you would have kicked him to the curb by now, too," Evan said. "Used his money for the *Excelsior* program and then fired him like you did me and Tim and everybody else."

He was closer to the truth than he knew. "He'll get what's coming to him."

"What are you up to, Dana? You're hiding something."

"We're all hiding something. Like your past."

"I've made peace with my mistakes."

"That's not true, and you know it. You carry your mistakes around with you everywhere you go. That soccer game." Dana knew the buttons that worked with Evan. That was the problem. The good men just weren't enough. They were too weak. Which left the world to people like McKnight. And her. She knew what she was.

"Jeez, I wish I was as perfect as you," Evan said.

"I've made my mistakes."

"Really?"

She turned away. There were things she knew better than to give away. Never show weakness. Never apologize. Even though she knew she owed Evan at least one apology. Going back to McKnight's bed had been a mistake. So maybe she owed him an answer after all.

Evan had almost disappeared in the bathroom door when Dana stopped him.

"Wait." She pulled from her pocket a folded-up piece of paper, and handed it to Evan. The picture showed a four-year-old boy. Evan flipped over the picture to read the words Dana knew by heart: Michael McKnight, December 5th, 1986.

"He was my son." She paused. "*Our* son." She looked at McKnight. "At least he was until about a year ago."

"I wanted to give the baby up for adoption, but Jack refused. That man can be a real bastard, but he really wanted to be a father. He took sole custody. I got my first job at DARPA and worked my way up to Director over the years."

"Michael died?" Evan scanned her face. "Did McKnight have anything to do with it?"

Dana gave McKnight a wicked glare.

"What are you planning, Dana?"

"Jack's been getting away with things his whole life. Not this time."

* * *

Three days later
Thessaloniki, Greece 4:15 am.

Evan hurried through the lobby of the hotel, duffel bags hanging from both shoulders, stuffed with food and gear. He saw a shuttle in the roundabout, loading its last passenger for the ride to Faros beach. Race volunteers had already transported his bike and cycling gear to the first transition area; likewise for his running gear, which would be brought to the second transition area in Sparta. Evan felt rested, but flustered. The race hadn't seemed real despite the pain of his preparations. It had just been a bridge to cross when he got to it. Now that the day had come, Evan couldn't stop thinking about what might happen in the race, whether he would finish, how well he would do.

Evan's breakfast had consisted of two slices of wheat bread with peanut butter and sliced bananas. A last chance to fuel up before the start. The shuttle driver made his last call for passengers, but Evan thought he had time to grab a Gatorade from his bag. As he reached into a pocket, the bag slipped off his shoulder and fell to the ground. Gu energy packets sprayed across the floor, and the Gatorade hit the ground and rolled toward the exit.

"Crap." Evan scurried after the rolling bottle. From a bent over position, he saw a foot stop the bottle's motion. Evan stood up to see his friend Tim Hacker standing over him.

Evan shot him a disbelieving stare, having not seen him in a year. He dropped his bags and gave Tim a hearty handshake. "Good to see you, man. What are you doing here?"

Tim opened the Gatorade, and handed Evan the bottle. "Every racer needs a support crew. I followed you from MIT. I decided to follow you to Greece as well."

The shuttle driver started the vehicle's engine.

"Truth be told, I needed a job," Tim said. "You were right about Dana. A month after she fired the research team, she let me go, too."

Evan shook his head. That sounded like Dana.

"Sorry, Tim." He watched the bus pull out of the driveway. "I have to catch this bus."

"Don't worry about it." Tim picked up Evan's duffel bag. "My car's over here."

* * *

Tim's Subaru Outback buzzed through the second largest city in Greece. From the passenger seat, Evan saw Byzantine and Roman-style architecture flash by, churches blurring into rows of houses, and the city's most famous landmark, the White Tower of Thessaloniki on the waterfront. They left the city and traveled down a main road on the easternmost section of the Halkidiki peninsula, lined with resorts, restaurants, and tourist attractions. The road hugged the coast, offering beautiful views of sandy beaches and secluded coves along the Aegean Sea. From small shacks built on the sand, the soft beat of rembetika music pulsed out. To the West were pine-forested hills and looping, rugged roads. They made their way south and the terrain became wilder, steep cliffs bordering the road.

As the drive went on, Evan had slipped into a focused state. Like Lucian had taught him, he began to visualize himself swimming gracefully, with a calm, perfect stroke. The drive also gave Evan and Tim time to catch up. Evan told his friend all about Lucian, the famous—or infamous, rather—Greek Olympian, and his year of brutal training, which included working out six days a week, no alcohol, no socializing… no life. They also talked about the Nan Air technology which they had been working on together at part of the *Excelsior* program.

"He's dead," Tim said.

"Who?"

"Dr. Weng."

Evan thought back to the day Weng visited DARPA, so proud that he'd solved the Grand Challenge of making respirocytes work safely. "Do you think Dana or McKnight had something to do with it? She was talking pretty crazy on the plane a few days ago."

"I don't know, but Weng didn't die of natural causes." Tim brought up a picture on his phone. It was a small black box with a thumb-sized red button. "Before Dana fired me, I took a picture of this in Dana's office."

"How'd you get in her office?"

"She went to that fancy Davos meeting in D.C., so that gave me time. As far as getting past the security, well... anyway, Dana's up to something, and I wasn't going to leave DARPA without some answers. I downloaded files from a folder in her encrypted files. As I was leaving, I saw this device tucked under some papers on her desk."

Evan studied the picture. The device looked like a remote control. "What is it?"

"Triggering device of some sort."

"For what?"

"Beats me... doesn't look friendly, though."

"What is Dana up to?"

"I don't know, Evan. But I think it's big."

Two

One year before
Arlington, Virginia
Defense Advanced Research Projects Agency (DARPA)

"Why do I always have to be the guinea pig?" Tim asked as he swung his leg into the hypobaric chamber, a seven-foot long tube made of glass that would soon simulate a low atmospheric pressure environment.

The human performance laboratory was stocked with state-of-the-art equipment to assess physiology and personal fitness. Monark cycle ergometers and treadmills stood in a neat row against one wall. Benches held lactate analyzers, electromyography, 12-lead EKGs, devices to measure body composition, and metabolic measurement systems.

"Don't worry, buddy." Evan sat behind a computer in the adjacent room. He always had to reassure Tim when it came to the experiments. "We've done this plenty of times."

"Not at this altitude," Tim said, shooting a concerned look into the room where Evan was sitting next to the Director of DARPA, Dana Brines.

"If the respirocytes work," Dana said, "you could be at the flying altitude of a passenger jet and you'd be fine."

"*If* they work," Tim said, stepping his other leg into the altitude chamber. "We haven't been able to get them yet."

Dana shrugged. "And that's why it's our Grand Challenge. There's a whole world out there of people who might be solving our problems for us."

Tim scanned the DARPA lab cautiously one last time before he reclined inside the glass chamber. "If someone creates a drug that's hundreds of times more efficient than biological blood, they're not going to call us; they're going to call Pfizer, or Genentech, and get stupidly rich." He latched the glass door closed. The microphones in the chamber still picked up his voice clearly. "Maybe they'll call Michael Phelps," Tim said, "see if he'd like to come out of retirement and shave a few *minutes* off his world records."

Beside Evan, Dana still seemed confident. "Whoever solves the Grand Challenge will come to us."

Tim spoke over the whir of vacuum pumps. "What makes you so sure?"

"Because the military pays better than pharmaceutical companies."

Evan had always had doubts about outsourcing the development of the Nan Airs through the Grand Challenge, a competition open to labs around the world. It felt strange to be waiting there for some stranger to simply drop the answer into their laps.

He returned his attention to Tim. Evan's training was as a limit physiologist, studying the effects of extreme environments on the human body. If the artificial red blood cells didn't work, simulating the height of Mount Everest would be especially dangerous for Tim's body. Only 100 people had summited the highest mountain in the world without the use of supplemental oxygen. The first to do so was mountaineer Reinhold Messner. Messner was a purist with strong objections to using artificial aid, yet despite the monumental achievement, even he said, "I am nothing more than a single narrow gasping lung, floating over the mists and summits."

Purity was not Evan's mandate at the most prominent research organization of the US Department of Defense, where he had come as a Fellow six months ago to run a purpose-built team. DARPA had an impressive record of innovation, including creating the internet's predecessor in 1969 and developing the precision navigation systems used in satellites, the Force F-117 Nighthawk (Stealth Fighter) and unmanned aerial vehicles (drones). Even with that track record, inventing artificial red blood cells that exponentially increased the human body's oxygen-carrying capacity was no small challenge. It was why Dana had created the Grand Challenge—spreading details of the core problem around the world, hoping to bring every available brain to bear on the issue and making it clear that the rewards would be there for anyone who solved it.

As an approach to scientific problems, it was one with a long record of success. Yet a part of Evan wanted to be the one to solve it. He and his team had been the ones putting in so much of the work, after all. Evan fiddled with the controls in front of him. He had told Tim that the respirocytes would work this time, but his confidence was a façade—manufactured to set his friend's mind at ease. The truth was that there was no way of knowing until they tested.

"Okay, buddy," Evan said. "Just lie back and we'll start the experiment."

Dana turned in her chair to face Evan. "Let's go to Everest."

Evan turned a dial slowly clockwise, reducing the concentration of oxygen in the glass chamber. Tim wrinkled his nose as he adjusted to the pressure change.

"We're at 10,000 feet," Evan said.

"I swear we have mice for tests like these," Tim complained.

"Pentagon officials are going to be here tomorrow," Dana said. "We've got to test the newest formulation on a human so that we have something to show them. Our funding depends on it. Anyway, what's the worst that could happen?"

"I could pass out, and then go into a coma and die?" Tim suggested.

It was no laughing matter for Evan. The height was well beyond the limits of normal physiology. Evan tried to set Tim's mind at ease. "We'll shut things down way before that happens, buddy."

The human body just wasn't made for such environmental extremes. But the altitude chamber was the best method of testing the respirocytes Dana had injected into Tim's arm minutes before he entered the chamber. As elevation increased, the concentration of oxygen in the atmosphere decreased, reducing the amount of oxygen that entered the blood and ultimately the cells. At 29,560 feet, the atmospheric pressure would be only 30% of that at sea level. If a sea-dweller were to be immediately transported to the summit of Everest, they would be unconscious within seconds, and would die after a few minutes.

And they were sending Tim up to that level. Tim Hacker was a brilliant nanotechnologist who specialized in engineering functional systems at the molecular scale. He was highly intellectual, though socially impaired. He was on the Autistic spectrum but claimed he didn't have Asperger's Syndrome. Social situations, such as dinners and outings with lab members, were painful for him, and he often skipped them to tinker in the lab. He had zero fashion sense and often wore baggy jeans, pulled up high. He was absolutely brilliant as well as loyal; Evan's right-hand-man. When Evan decided to leave MIT for DARPA, Tim had followed without hesitation.

Before Evan arrived at DARPA, respirocytes were purely hypothetical, a dream of *Nanomedicine* author Rob Freitas, who created conceptual designs for the artificial red blood cells about the size of a micron, or one millionth of a meter. When the diameter of a human hair was about 40-50 microns thick, working on that scale presented its own challenges. The Pentagon had asked DARPA Director Dana Brines to oversee the *Excelsior* program with the ambitious aim of bringing Freitas' technology to life. Theoretically, one respirocyte could carry 236 times more oxygen and carbon dioxide than a natural red blood cell. If the nanotechnological devices worked, they would enable a person to sprint at full speed for several minutes without taking a breath, or remain underwater for a couple minutes on a single breath.

"Okay, we're at 20,000 feet, Tim," Evan said. "That's Everest basecamp. How're you feeling?"

"Lightheaded," Tim said. His voice was weak, the words barely coming.

Dana shook her head. "If the Nan Airs were working…"

"He would be able to sing the National Anthem right now," Evan said.

"Let's just go a bit more," Dana said. "I know what I'm doing."

She sounded completely in control of the situation, just as she always did. Just as she'd been late in the lab one night when she walked straight up to him, grabbed him by the lab coat, and kissed him. Their relationship, if you could call it that, always took place on her terms. It wasn't just that she was the boss. It was that she was willing to go out and take what she wanted.

Evan wondered what she saw in him, a postdoctoral scientist fresh out of MIT. He was a junior scientist; she was the leader of a staff of almost 300

personnel in charge of a budget of nearly $3 billion. She was a physical speci-
men who ran five miles every morning and swam in pools in the night. Evan's
muscles had atrophied after years of doctoral work at lab benches.

Dana leaned in fearlessly and kissed the back of Evan's neck. She began
massaging his neck and his worries melted away, concerns such as whether he
would be able to get his $1.6 million research project to work, as well as the
experiment in the adjacent room and Tim's drifting consciousness.

Evan closed his eyes as Dana rubbed his shoulders. He remembered when
his shoulders had been sturdier, his body stronger. Six years ago, his stomach
had been flat, not flabby like it was now. He had been in nearly perfect physical shape when he was a hopeful for the Olympic soccer team. He used to look
in the mirror and see a trim body and ripped muscles. Now he saw underde-
veloped pectorals and skinny arms. He always regretted leaving soccer after
"the incident," especially since he thought he had made the right choice on the
field, an honest one. While he was proud to have earned a PhD in physiology,
he had always considered his physical decline shameful.

Evan heard Tim's distressed voice, and it seemed to come from a long way
away. "Um, Evan? I'm a little woozy here."

Dana didn't seem concerned, even though the atmospheric pressure inside
the chamber was 40% the concentration of oxygen at sea level.

"We're at 25,000 feet," Evan said. "It's clear the respirocytes aren't work–"

"Oh, c'mon," Dana said. "We can do this." She turned the dial clockwise
further.

Evan looked past her. The EKG monitoring Tim's heart rate displayed 198
beats per minute. "His pulse is skyrocketing."

Tim's respiration had increased, to 25 breaths per minute. Through the
glass, Evan saw Tim's face pinch in pain. At just 13,000 feet, nearly half of the
people started to develop symptoms of acute mountain sickness, a condition
characterized by headache, nausea, dizziness, fatigue, and insomnia. Tim was
way past that now.

Evan started for the controls. "He's going to pass out."

Dana covered his hand with hers. "He's got an emergency oxygen bottle,
if anything happens. But we need the data."

Tim let out a garbled string of words. He dragged his fingers along the glass in a stupor, his eyes glossed over. Tim was experiencing a simulated altitude of 26,000, a height known as "the death zone." Above that altitude, the human body could no longer adapt to low oxygen levels. Bodily functions deteriorated, and the risk of pulmonary edema started to set in, the lungs filling with fluid. Cerebral edema, or water in the brain, typically followed, then coma, then death if not returned to sea level.

Tim lunged for the emergency oxygen mask clumsily, but couldn't grasp the handle. His eyes rolled back, and then he lost consciousness.

"He's passing out," Evan said. He pushed Dana aside, lunged for the dial, and gave it a strong turn counterclockwise. He watched the altitude drop from 26,000 feet to 20,000 then 15,500. Tim's eyes opened at 12,000 feet. He found enough strength to punch the glass.

"Get me the *hell* out of here!"

The phone rang next to Evan.

Dana stood. "I'll go help Tim. Would you mind getting the phone?"

Evan answered while Dana went over to Tim.

"This is Evan," he said.

"Dr. Galloway, this is security at the front desk. There's a man here who wants to see Dr. Brines."

Evan looked over to where Dana was checking on Tim. Now that the experiment was done, she tended to him with a brisk sort of care, but a glance back in Evan's direction made it clear that she wanted to know what was going on.

Evan wanted to know too. This was a government facility. People didn't just walk in off the street, as a rule.

"She's busy right now. It will have to be important."

"The man who came in says that it is," the security guard said. "His name is Dr. Weng."

Evan tried to place the man but couldn't. "I've never heard of him. Why are you calling this through?"

"Because he claims that he's solved Dr. Brines' Grand Challenge."

Three

Faros beach, Greece

The beach was normally a quiet sliver of sand jutting out into the Thermaic Gulf, deserted except for a few locals, not quite beautiful enough for the tourists. For the ultra-triathlon, however, it was swarming with spectators and reporters. They crowded the sand, held back by little more than lines of tape. The reporters crossed them regularly, interviewing athletes and talking into cameras. It was only 7:30 am, but loud techno music blared from a lively volunteer tent. Between songs, an animated DJ yelled words of encouragement as well as details about the course and the weather. Apparently, due to heavy rains throughout the night, the water's temperature had dropped from 64 degrees Fahrenheit to 51.

It would be a cold swim, Evan thought, as he applied Body Glide to his body, which would allow him to slip out of his wetsuit quickly at the transition area. He had also rubbed Vaseline around his crotch, under his armpits, and over his nipples to prevent chaffing. He pulled his Aquasphere wetsuit up and over his chest and then pulled the string behind his back to close the suit. While the water was chilly, the air temperature was 75 degrees, which made wearing the wetsuit uncomfortable while standing there. He looked toward the choppy water; some athletes were warming up with short practice swims. He saw Tim on a paddleboard gliding away from the beach. As the sole member of Evan's support crew, Tim would keep an eye on Evan as he swam. He would alert the safety boats if Evan was in trouble.

"You need a number," Isabella Dawson said from the side.

Evan was happy to see her, but he shook his head, confused. "Number?"

She pointed to his thigh. "Your *race* number." She giggled, and darted off. "Follow me to body marking."

Evan followed Isabella as she cut through hordes of people. Her wetsuit wasn't fully zipped up, which exposed a tight-fitting, black sports bra. It was almost unfair how gorgeous her body was. Athletic, but slender; muscular, but trim—exactly the body type that made Evan weak in the knees. The papers were calling Isabella "the woman of steel." She had started life as a world-class rock climber from Grenada, Spain. Widely considered the most successful female climber of her time, she had won three world championship titles and five victories at the Rock Masters competition in Arco, Italy. When she had wanted a different kind of challenge, she began competing in triathlons and had won several.

Isabella pointed to a registration table lined with volunteers. Evan barely pulled his eyes from her body before she spun around. She gave Evan a smile that said she knew exactly what he'd been doing. "Let's hope you concentrate better during the triathlon." Isabella turned around and bunched her hair up. "Would you mind zipping up my wetsuit, please?"

"Um… yes, of course," Evan said. He grabbed the zipper with one hand and pushed downward on the suit with the other. As he pulled the zipper up, he tried to be polite and avert his eyes, but they were drawn to Isabella's soft neck and brown, flowing hair—

"Gracias," Isabella said, with a grin. "Now, from here on out, you'd better concentrate. We're competitors."

"Let's just hope you can keep up." Evan narrowed his eyes playfully, and strolled to the registration table. He liked Isabella's spirit. She was playful, but also fierce—strong-willed and competitive enough to dominate women's rock climbing, not to mention the steel it took just to participate in a 700-mile ultra-triathlon.

"Name?" the volunteer said a second time.

Evan started. "Um… Galloway, Evan."

Isabella chuckled at his side.

The volunteer flipped through notecards. "Race number 15?" She pursed her lips. "Last one to register, huh?"

Evan nodded, remembering the night he had registered for the *Aletheia* a year ago, perhaps the world's most high-profile act of insanity. It was the same night he had caught Dana in bed with McKnight. He visited a couple bars after storming out of her house that night, and telling McKnight that he would participate in his race. It had taken a couple shots of tequila and a handful of beers before he brought himself to register for the 700-mile triathlon over the phone.

"*Numero uno* in my book," Isabella said lightheartedly. Then she flashed a smile and strode away. "See you out there, Evan."

Evan squeezed the contents of a Gu packet into his mouth as another race volunteer used a black magic marker to draw the number 15 on his right leg and arm.

Four

Arlington Country, Virginia

Dana puffed a cigarette to life, and then handed it to McKnight. He had just returned from the marathon in China. She hadn't slept with McKnight since they were in their twenties. The few recent minutes of sex had been a mistake. He was good in bed, but it opened too many old scars. The son he had taken custody of as an infant hung between them, impossible for Dana to ignore. If it weren't for the chance to avenge the adult son's death, she wouldn't have done it at all.

When they had first discussed the marathon on the Great Wall of China, McKnight had said that he was going to give the test-grade respirocytes to a local runner—someone he could coerce or buy-off. She had followed the race in the newspapers. When she had read that Michael had died, she was surprised by how devastated she had been. She had always prided herself on being so strong, emotionless. She didn't leave her bed for a day after she had learned the news.

The decision to kill McKnight had been an easy one. An obvious one, given what he had done. The only question had been how. Getting close to him had been easy. He never loved anyone but himself, yet he still found her attractive. Dana could have plunged a knife into him at any time tonight.

But using the respirocytes would be better. He should die as her son had died. His magnum opus—the ultra-triathlon he had named the *Aletheia*—would be his last race. It was the only form of vengeance that truly fit.

Yet there was something that *didn't* fit. Next to McKnight, she couldn't help thinking of Evan. They were too different for it to ever really work. As Director of DARPA, she led one of the most advanced arms of the United States government, and rubbed shoulders with four-star generals. Evan was a research fellow who haunted the lab with nerdy grad students. Last week she had approved plans for a hypersonic airplane that flew at twenty-times the speed of sound; Evan developed iPhone apps with Tim in his spare time. He was too nice for it ever to be more than a brief moment or two between them.

It had been difficult to witness Evan and Tim try hundreds of times to create safe respirocytes, even though they had found the correct design in only a few weeks. She had been manipulating their data, because, in fact, she was managing two projects under DARPA's *Excelsior* program, which called for a second Nan Air prototype. Evan and his Human Performance team were only aware of the first project—an agenda to create a functioning respirocytes, but the Pentagon had also asked for a version of Nan Airs that could be used to kill, if necessary. It was this project that Dana had outsourced through the Grand Challenge. It was McKnight's resources and Dr. Weng's brains that made it happen.

Dr. Weng had found a clever way to harmonize an electromagnetic pulse (EMP) with the Nan Airs. Sent from a small hand-held remote control, the EMP destroyed the Nan Airs, breaking them apart in the bloodstream. The immune system then recognized the disintegrated nano-devices as a severe infection, which resulted in flushed skin, fever, altered mental status, hyper-ventilation, low blood pressure, and eventually systemic inflammation, organ failure, and death. Dana had made sure that Evan stayed unaware of this second agenda, focused entirely on creating the first respirocyte prototype, which he had done quite early on.

McKnight blew wispy smoke rings into the air. "You know, when Michael was a boy, he used to love Achilles. He would dress up like him, run around the house sword-fighting, quoting from the *Iliad*." McKnight blew out more smoke. McKnight continued, more solemn. "You know it wasn't supposed to happen the way it did in China. Weng said he could control the immune response."

Dana wasn't listening to McKnight. She was too busy thinking about the implications of her work. The summer Olympics would take place in Greece in a year, and athletes and coaches had gotten wind of Dana's Nan Air technology. They were already trying to get them, trying to get any edge they could. She had been receiving non-stop phone calls from ravenous athletes and coaches seeking the technology. Some athletes had even showed up at her doorstep at DARPA, demanding whatever they could get.

The decision came to her like the shifting of silent gears in the dark. She stared up at the ceiling, thinking through the details, but the core of it came to her whole, intact. She questioned it, of course, but the heart of it was simple: the athletes deserved to pay as much as McKnight did. If they hadn't created such a demand for chemical edges, then the research would have stayed purely military. Its test subjects would all have been military personnel, and McKnight would never have become involved. If professional sportspeople had been half as pure as they pretended, her son might still be alive.

There had to be a price for that.

Five

"What the hell happened while I was in that chamber, man?" Tim asked. He and Evan followed Dana down the hallway to the Human Performance laboratory. Dana was giving the Chinese scientist, Dr. Kevin Weng, a tour of the facility.

Evan hesitated. "Yeah, sorry about that, I—"

"Fell asleep at the wheel, is what you did." Tim shook his head. "That could have been a lot worse, man. I have a *wicked* headache right now."

The group passed by the Body Composition laboratory, where a postdoctoral researcher holding an iPad connected to a *BodPod* was testing a man in military uniform, a soldier from a local base.

"Ever heard of this Dr. Weng?" Evan asked.

Tim shook his head. "While we waited for his security clearance, I did a quick search on PubMed for him. He's not published anywhere in the literature. I couldn't even find where he got his PhD."

"And yet he says he's solved one of the greatest modern-day engineering challenges?"

Tim smirked. "So he says."

"The day before the Pentagon visit, too." Evan couldn't help being suspicious. "That's convenient."

"If he solved the Grand Challenge," Tim said, walking through a glass door, "I wonder where that leaves us."

"What do you mean?"

"I mean, Dana brought us here to develop respirocytes. If someone else developed them, doesn't that put us out of a job?"

"Dana would never do that."

Dana had always given Evan the impression that he was DARPA's golden boy, and always told him how talented she thought he was—how she wanted him to stay long after the *Excelsior* project ended. When she had visited MIT, she had seemed overwhelmed with Evan's scientific achievements. Not even a PhD recipient then, Evan had already been published in prestigious journals, including *Science, Nature* and *Cell*. He had also won the prestigious National Institutes of Health (NIH) Director's Early Independence Award. His advisor, a world-renowned biophysicist, called him the most impressive doctoral student he had ever mentored.

Dana was originally attracted to Evan's research on developing a genetic test that could predict vulnerability to altitude sickness. At the time, there was still no way of knowing who would succumb to altitude sickness. Age, gender, and even physical fitness couldn't predict whether someone would fall sick. Evan had discovered that susceptibility was fundamentally genetic, a result of five specific genes. He developed a blood test that could predict who would fall ill with 97% accuracy. The test caught the attention of the military, who couldn't predict which soldiers would succumb to altitude sickness when deployed in high altitude battlefields. Even the fittest soldiers could fall prey, debilitated by headaches, nausea, and dizziness. Military models showed that 25-35% of troops experienced altitude sickness at 10,000 feet. At 13,200 feet, that number rose to 80-90%. Because altitude drugs were expensive, and carried undesirable side effects, the military licensed Evan's tests.

Ahead of him and Tim, Dana shot Weng a smile. "Down the hall is our Human Performance laboratory, Dr. Weng. With the latest technology in exercise science, we can measure fuel utilization to pinpoint a soldier's optimal fat-burning intensity during exercise; resting metabolic rate to—"

"I hate to interrupt the tour, Dr. Brines," Dr. Weng said abruptly, "but I'd like to discuss the respirocyte technology."

"Of course." Dana led Weng down the hall. "Right this way."

Weng was unkempt, his hair disheveled, and he wore a tacky sweater and slacks that could have been from the 1970s. Evan thought the scientist seemed arrogant as well, one of those scientists who carried the attitude of being burdened. It wouldn't be the first time that a lone wolf had shifted a paradigm.

Tim walked in-step with Weng. "So where are you stationed?"

"New York."

"What university?"

"Private sector."

"Right," Tim said, glancing at Evan. "Certainly pays better."

"Indeed it does."

Dana pointed to a sign that read, *Human Performance Lab.* "Here we are." She looked at Evan. "Well, this is usually where I turn it over to Dr. Galloway, our limit physiologist."

Evan recognized his cue. "I study the human body at extreme environmental conditions: hot, cold, high pressure, low pressure, high altitude, varying g-forces, microgravity."

"Considering the narrow range of environments humans can live in, I always thought the body was quite fragile," Weng said.

"Actually, humans are rather extraordinary in their ability to adapt to environmental conditions. The Eskimos have lived successfully in arctic wastelands. The Pygmies of Central Africa survive in humid rainforests. And the people of the Tibetan Plateau live at 14,763 feet."

Weng asked, "But isn't there a good deal of variance in how efficiently people can tolerate environmental extremes?"

Evan folded his hands behind his back. "Did you ever read comic books as a child, Dr. Weng?"

"Um, yes, like most children, I suppose."

"Maybe you remember Steven Rogers?"

Weng thought for a moment. "Captain America?"

"That's right," Evan said.

Weng said, "If I remember, he was *quite* disadvantaged."

"Rogers couldn't enlist in the military during World War II because he was frail and unathletic. But the US government recruited him for a secret program. They injected him with an experimental serum that gave him speed, stamina, and strength, greater than even the most elite Olympic athlete. He was transformed into the picture of athletic perfection, a physical specimen." Evan opened the double doors to the Human Performance lab. "This is the premise for the *Excelsior* program, built around the respirocyte technology, which we call Nan Airs."

Weng tilted his head. "A field we have in common."

Evan strolled into the enormous lab space. "DARPA has scientists working on information technology, cognitive neuroscience, and biological engineering. In my lab, we focus mainly on nanotechnology-based technology."

"The *final* frontier," Tim said in a sarcastic tone.

"You will have to excuse Dr. Hacker," Dana said. "Brilliant technologist; doesn't have the best manners, though."

Tim said, "I just wonder if these advances are too far ahead of our ability to deal with ethical consequences."

Evan didn't want to be drawn into the conversation. He didn't have his mind made up on the matter. If his father were still alive, the former minister certainly wouldn't agree with the *Excelsior* program. Did Evan care? No. Perhaps that's why he had signed up in the first place.

Weng asked, "What are you so afraid of Dr. Hacker?"

Tim looked over at the other scientist, the challenge obvious. "What if we lose what it means to be human?"

Evan decided to change the subject. He pointed to a row of treadmills. "On these state-of-the-art treadmills, we can simulate stop-and-go maneuvers. The ones without a platform are force treadmills, where we have soldiers wear a belt to stay in place. Then we use a potentiometer to adjust the load they carry from zero to 100 pounds." Evan grabbed the rail of a treadmill. Running on it was a soldier wearing a bulky facemask, which fit snugly over his mouth and nose. Tubes from the mask fed back to a desktop computer with a large LCD screen. "We're doing VO2max testing, a measure of aerobic fitness. We'll have this cadet sprint anywhere from 5 to 60 seconds, and then we can measure his oxygen consumption, as well as assess sub-max V02 and anaerobic threshold."

"Over here we conduct vision training," Evan said, moving to another station. "The Air Force used to use it to improve the performance of fighter pilots. We use it to enhance hand-eye coordination and depth perception in combat soldiers."

Evan swept his arm toward the corner of the room. "We also perform Wingate testing to measure power. And over there we conduct dual energy X-ray absorptiometry to determine fat and lean body mass."

He was killing time and he knew it. He both wanted to see what Weng had come up with and didn't, because the moment the other scientist demonstrated that he had indeed solved the Grand Challenge, Evan's efforts on the project were for nothing. The main focus of his life at DARPA had been solving this problem, and to have it swept away by someone coming in from nowhere just felt wrong.

Dana seemed to be more eager though. "Thank you, Evan. Basically, we're commissioned by the Pentagon to create the ultimate soldier. Dr. Galloway and Dr. Hacker have been stumped by the Nan Air technology, so we're naturally intrigued by what you have to offer, Dr. Weng."

"Before I show you my design," Weng said, placing his briefcase on a desk, "might I ask how you intend to announce the winner?"

Dana looked taken aback, but she was polite. "We usually make an announcement internally, and then—"

"I'd like your public relations department to see that my discovery is publicized in the popular press, including *The New York Times, Forbes,* and *Newsweek.* If you can't do that, I will have to think about going elsewhere."

Evan was repulsed by the directness of that demand. Weng wanted the fame, and all the bells and whistles that came with a game-changing technology. Weng probably wanted his own *Nova* special, too.

Dana looked eager to please, however. "I'm sure we can make that happen, Dr. Weng. Now, the technology please."

Weng snapped open his briefcase and pulled out an iPad. He accessed a video and pressed play. The group huddled around as Weng oriented them.

"You're looking at a 21-year-old male running a marathon on the Great Wall of China."

Evan was flabbergasted. "You tested the respirocytes in a *public* marathon?"

"My partner and I wanted to test them in the field."

The video showed a runner skip up large granite steps effortlessly. Weng said, "At the moment, he's over an hour ahead of the second-place runner."

Evan looked at Dana and was surprised to see her distraught. Her lips quivered ever so slightly. Did she have tears in her eyes?

Tim pointed at the screen. "I know that guy. He was a runner for the USA track and field team." Tim frowned. "Guy was banned from running professionally for doping."

"We knew of his past, obviously," Weng said. "But we had to recruit someone who could embrace, shall we say… moral ambiguity."

"Someone who didn't mind cheating," Evan said.

"*Evan.*" Dana turned to Weng. "Dr. Galloway worries that this technology could get into everyday sports. But of course, it's for military use only."

That didn't sound likely. Evan couldn't shake the idea that, as a species, humans seemed to be designed to game the system. Perhaps the tendency to exploit, to cheat, couldn't be overcome. On Wall Street, high-frequency traders rigged the market, chemical companies tweaked compounds to design drugs that evade laws, and Big Food companies lobbied the government for subsidies to ensure the USDA's nutritional recommendations worked in their favor. The ambitious athletes of the world, willing to do anything for an edge, for the almighty win, would flock to respirocytes if they could get them.

Weng smiled slightly. "While I think it's a noble ideal to keep sports pure, frankly, I think you're kidding yourself, Dr. Galloway. Modern-day sports are already rife with these cheaters. The dam has burst." Weng paused, and then went on. "Indeed, the line between the artificial and the pure is hardly a clear thing. Athletes strengthen their muscles with sophisticated weight lifting machines. They take painkillers for back pain, creatine and protein shakes after workouts. These are forms of enhancements, in my opinion, and yet they're all legal."

Evan didn't have a good answer. "It's just not right."

"Dr. Galloway," Weng said, "you're not exactly doing the purest research in the world."

Evan frowned, but held back his response to that. "You have data to show the results of your work? And your methods?"

"Of course," Dr. Weng said. He tapped the iPad. "It's all in here."

"You're working with a partner, right? When do we get to meet him?"

Weng rubbed the back of his neck, the small movement surprisingly anxious. "My partner would like to remain anonymous."

Dana placed a hand on Weng's back. "Well, I guess that doesn't matter. Not if you have the answers we have all been looking for. I would like to formally invite you to our quarterly meeting with the Pentagon tomorrow. It'll give you a chance to get a little of that recognition you're looking for."

As Dana and Weng turned to leave, Tim interrupted. "Where is he now?"

"Who?" Weng asked, confused.

"You're marathon runner."

Weng shrugged. "Oh, he's recovering."

Six

Faros Beach, Greece 7:55 am.

Five minutes until the triathlon began. Evan waded into the shallow water with the other triathletes. Everyone was edgy; focused, but tense. Evan tasted salt as sea water sprayed into his face. The water was choppy from strong winds whipping across the beach, and waves shoved him back as he moved toward the middle of the pack.

Evan could barely see the patch of land to which they were going to be swimming twelve miles away. It was customary to have the fastest swimmers at the front. Evan positioned himself in the second row. Lucian had taught him to get behind a fast swimmer and swim in their slipstream. He saw his brother at the front of the pack. Evan moved in behind him, wanting to wish him good luck. "Hey, Luke, I just wanted to say—"

A race volunteer spoke through loudspeaker. "Welcome everyone to the *2015 Aletheia Ultra*. Please join me as we play the Greek national anthem."

Luke put his hand over his heart, ignoring Evan.

"You're planning to ignore me all race?" Evan demanded. "I know you did a pretty good job during the whole year of training, but that's pushing it."

Luke didn't look healthy. He was pale, twitchy. Was he using drugs again? He had lost fifty pounds in rehab, and would tell anyone who listened that his new, slender body was a blessing, since he now carried less weight in triathlons. Evan leaned in closer. "Luke—"

"I know why you're here," Luke said. The music from the loudspeaker was loud, nearly drowning out his voice. "You're here because you caught Jack screwing your girlfriend."

Luke was on a first name basis with Jack McKnight? That was enough to make Evan pause. Should he tell his brother the real reason? That he also signed up to look after him? No, that wouldn't go over well. Luke had never appreciated Evan's attempts to protect him. Not with the drugs. Not with anything.

"Just wanted to wish you good luck."

"Just stay out of my way out there. Triathlon is my event. You should have stuck to soccer."

Evan had spoken with Luke around the time that McKnight had announced the *Aletheia* to the world on television. He'd wanted to check that his brother was okay. Luke was an adrenaline junkie—what scientists liked to call a "high sensation seeker." He was ready to take physical, social, legal, and financial risks for the sake of any new and exciting experience. If it wasn't the booze or the cocaine, it was gambling or extreme sports, like base jumping or extreme skiing. Inevitably, Luke's recklessness had caught up to him. He'd spent six months in rehabilitation, then 18 months in Boston's Federal Correctional Institute. Evan had wanted to check that his brother was still staying away from the drugs.

"Look, Luke," Evan had said, "this triathlon isn't for you."

Luke had been defiant. "You can cool it with the big brother crap, Ev."

Evan knew there was little anyone could do or say after Luke committed to something. Luke was similar to him in that respect. There had always been that same competitiveness, self-reliance, and high ambition in both of them. In Luke, however, it too often turned into obsession. Luke considered it all part of a rehabilitated "brand new Luke." For him, the race wins and the extreme sports were a symbol of the new man he'd become.

In Evan's opinion, Luke hadn't broken his addictive habits—he had simply replaced his drug of choice with ultra-running endurance races. Even so, Evan had to at least make an attempt to stop his brother.

"You heard what experts said about the *Aletheia*," Evan had said. "Even if you could finish, you'll probably end up destroying your body in the process. I'm a physiologist for God's sake, when are you going to listen to me?"

Luke had laughed at that. "You scientists think you know it all, until someone comes along and does the impossible. Then you scramble to rewrite your little papers. They said the four-minute mile would kill whoever did it. I think you're just jealous. Jealous that I might actually win, and challenge you as Dad's golden boy."

Evan had paused at that. Was there any truth to that? Evan had certainly been the star soccer player in Boston when they were kids, and he'd had every intention of becoming a professional player after college. The sport had come naturally to him. Luke, on the other hand, had gravitated toward track, but a range of physical ailments, such as back pain, stomach conditions, and even bouts of depression had held Luke back as a boy.

Evan had known that Luke was jealous of his abilities and athletic success. Evan had long enjoyed his "can-do-no-wrong" leadership position, deciding what the two of them should do, guiding his brother's decisions. Perhaps Luke was right. Perhaps that was why it had been hard for Evan to watch his brother's recent success in the endurance racing circuit.

Luke had run his first ultra-running race before he went to jail. Known as the "world's toughest footrace," he competed in the legendary Badwater ultramarathon, a 135-mile run through the salt flats of Death Valley, ending 8,000 feet above sea level at the top of Mount Whitney, the highest point in the United States. It took place in July, the hottest month in an already brutal environment. Some days the temperature reached 120 degrees Fahrenheit. When Evan visited Luke in jail, Luke proclaimed he would leave jail stronger than before, and would starting winning ultra-events. To Evan's surprise, he had made good on that promise many times over.

"I'm not jealous," Evan eventually said then. "I'm just looking out for you."

Luke shook his head at that. "You always got the best grades, the prettiest girls. You even got a doctorate. Now it's time for me to get the spotlight."

"Luke, you're still recovering—"

"*Recovered.*"

"Fine, recovered," Evan said, hoping to pacify his brother. "Don't you think you should take it easy, though? You've barely been out a year."

"I wanted your support." Luke's tone was adversarial. "Thanks for nothing."

* * *

Evan pushed the memory aside. It wasn't easy. It nagged at him, but he moved to the periphery, took a deep breath, and started his preparation ritual in the water. He covered his head with a rubber swimming cap and then swung his arms to loosen his shoulders. He splashed water on his chest and then his face. The water was chilly, but refreshing. It probably wasn't going to be too refreshing after seven hours of swimming in it, though. Evan swiveled his head and caught Isabella's eyes. She winked and then put on her swim cap as well.

McKnight's voice came from behind Evan. "You look fit," he said. "I'm impressed."

Evan peered out of the corner of his eye at the other man. "Fit enough."

McKnight looked to be in absolutely exquisite shape. There had been a *New York Times* article about him and his "mind-bendingly" difficult training program. Apparently he hadn't restricted himself to endurance races in his preparation. Reporters followed him around like mosquitoes, interviewing McKnight after free solo rock climbs in Yosemite, or hundred-mile running races. He'd entered weightlifting competitions and judo tournaments, cycling events and rowing regattas. There were times when it had looked like McKnight had been determined to show off the effects of his respirocyte-fueled body in as many environments as possible. Maybe that was the point. Maybe he was planning on being his own advertisement for his product. Or maybe he just wanted to win as many different things as possible, regardless of how he did it.

McKnight was the fittest looking of Evan's opponents, but not by as much as Evan might have thought. Evan was in the best shape of his life, but he felt out of his league next to the fifteen competitors around him. McKnight looked more like a Greek God than an endurance athlete. McKnight had stacked on perhaps twenty pounds of lean muscle, and his body didn't have a loose piece of skin on it.

McKnight chuckled. "Fit enough? We'll see."

"I'm fit enough to beat you," Evan said, keeping his eyes on the horizon.

"You're really going to have to learn the hard way, aren't you?"

McKnight slapped Luke on the back. "It was a good year of training, buddy. You ready?"

"Of course I'm ready," Luke said, with a look back at Evan.

The man with the loudspeaker lifted a gun to the sky. "Aletheian's, get ready."

Evan stared at the two of them. They had trained together? Who knew what that piece of garbage had told his brother? Or given him? That was the biggest fear. The one that tightened in Evan's chest like a fist. The one he had to push aside, because there was no more time. The loudspeaker blared again.

"Ready!"

McKnight didn't look bothered. "You're looking at the winner and the runner-up here. We'll know which one is which in about three days."

Evan glared at McKnight. "At the end of this race, the world will know something, alright."

"*On your mark…*"

McKnight said, "And what's that?"

"*Get set…*"

"That there are no shortcuts," Evan said. "And that character is more important than outcome."

"*Go!*"

The gun fired, and Evan dove headfirst into the churning water.

Seven

As Evan cut through the water, he let his mind drift, taking it away from the efforts of his muscles, the rhythmic taking in of air every couple of strokes. He found himself drifting back to the night he caught Dana and McKnight in bed together. He had stood on Dana's doorstep that night, shaking the rain from his umbrella. He set the bottle of Italian sparkling wine on the railing of the deck, and rummaged through his pocket for his keys. There was a black Audi A7 in the driveway. He hoped it wasn't a Pentagon official, as he wasn't in the entertaining mood. He had bought the bottle of Prosecco to Dana's house to celebrate, because they finally had a prototype to show the army. He'd also planned to finish what Dana started during the experiment. Evan found the key, unlocked the door, and walked into the foyer. The lights were dim in the house, and apart from the television playing in the living room, all was quiet.

Dana always insisted that Evan come to her house. Dana's house was in Arlington, the richest county in America. Her 9,000-square-foot colonial home had five bedrooms, a pool, and spectacular views of the Potomac River. Evan could only afford a small apartment in Crystal City, just south of downtown Washington, D.C.

"Hello?" Evan threw his jacket over a chair. He walked into the kitchen and set the bottle down. "I come bearing gifts."

Would he catch her on the elliptical in the living room, in her tight yoga pants, sweaty from working out? He wandered into the living room, and saw the elliptical unplugged, Dana's jacket hanging from the handlebars. He thought he smelled smoke, but it was faint, barely noticeable.

The television was playing a special on ESPN. It looked like a recap of a softball game. The noise of it covered everything else in the room.

"And now, for the #1 act of sportsmanship in our series, we look back at the 2008 softball game between the University of Western Oregon and Central Washington University." Evan watched as a young woman stepped up to the plate. There were two runners on base. She let a pitch go past her for a strike. The next pitch, she swung hard and sent the softball soaring over the centerfield fence. She began rounding the bases, but in her excitement, she failed to touch first base.

"Realizing her mistake," the sportscaster continued, "Sara Tucholsky turns back to first base, but in doing so badly twists her knee." Evan cringed as the young woman fell to the ground in agony, gripping her knee. She crawled toward first base. "The first base coach tells her that she would be called out if her teammates tried to help her; the umpire tells her a pinch runner will have to be called in, and the home run will count as a single."

Then two players from the opposing team rushed toward the injured player. The members of the Central Washington softball team picked up Tucholsky and carried her around the bases, making the three-run homer count. In doing so, Central Washington lost the game and was eliminated from the playoffs. The camera panned through the crowd, and spectators from both teams were cheering, some were tearing up over the display of sportsmanship.

If only other sports were that way, Evan thought. There was a time when he'd applaud such behavior, but he knew stuff like that didn't happen anymore. Now it was all about winning. These days, sportsmanship didn't reward athletes; it alienated them.

Evan heard a thud through the ceiling. He darted across the living room, grabbed the wine and hurried up the stairs toward Dana's room. He passed pictures in the stairwell of Dana smiling with Senators, the President of the United States, and of course, lieutenant general Edwin Somervell, to whom they would present their data tomorrow.

As he got closer, it sounded like Dana was crying. "It was the biggest mistake of my life leaving Michael with you."

"You wanted a career, not a child," a man's voice said. "What does it matter now, anyway?"

Evan swung open the door to Dana's room. Dana threw a blanket over her naked body. To Evan's horror, her clothes were strewn across the floor, and an opened bottle of wine sat on the nightstand.

Dana wrapped the sheet around her chest and leapt off the bed. She dried her eyes and pointed her palm at Evan defensively. "Evan, listen—"

Jack McKnight marched out of the bathroom in a bathrobe. A cigar hung from his lips.

Evan didn't know what to do or say.

"What the hell is he doing here?" McKnight asked, snatching the cigar from his mouth.

Evan backpedaled slowly, his fists clenched. A part of him wanted to attack McKnight, but he was overmatched. He thought about running, but didn't want to look like a coward. Instead, he stood and pointed his finger at McKnight, shaking with rage.

"I'll see you in that race of yours."

Eight

Evan and Tim walked toward the lab's break room, sidestepping a team of sharply dressed professionals, gripping briefcases and boxes, bulldozing their way down the hallway. Evan recognized one of the men from DARPA's legal department. One woman, Cynthia, worked in human resources. Dana was holding up the rear, speaking rapidly and making forceful gestures.

"We'll do this after the Pentagon meeting…"

Evan looked across to Tim. "What's all that about?"

The brigade of professionals flooded into a conference room.

"I don't know." Tim's eye flitted from person to person. "A conference room packed with lawyers and HR is never a good thing."

Dana walked into the room last, closed the door, and drew the shades.

Evan and Tim headed for the break room. Tim grabbed two coffee mugs and slid one under a Keurig coffee maker. He placed a K-cup pod into the machine and pressed a button; the machine squirted coffee after a few seconds.

"Cream?"

"Sure." Evan seated himself at a round table. Tim opened the refrigerator and rummaged around. Tim's shirt caught the edge of a milk jug and knocked it to the floor. As he leaned down to pick it up, he hit the opening of a 12-pack of Coca Cola cans. Two of the carbonated drinks tumbled to the floor before he could plug the opening with a hand.

Tim was the clumsiest person Evan had ever met. "Well, that was four days without an incident," Evan said. "A good week."

Evan stood up and repositioned the cardboard box on the refrigerator, securing the cans.

Tim retrieved two cans from the floor and walked them to the sink. "Ever heard of a man named Thales?" he said, fully cracking open the can of soda in the sink. Fizz and bubbles sprayed as the carbon dioxide escaped.

"He was a philosopher, right?"

Tim tossed the can into the trash. Evan grabbed it and placed it into the recycle container.

Tim chuckled. "Always the Boy Scout."

"You were saying."

"Right. Thales *was* a philosopher, the first we know of." Tim put another K-cup into the coffee maker. "The Greeks hailed Thales as the founder of science, mathematics, and philosophy. He was also an astronomer. Plato told a story about Thales. One night Thales was strolling quietly, studying the stars. He was so engrossed in thought, so captivated by the sky above that he didn't notice a well at his feet, and he fell in."

"Sounds like someone I know," Evan said, chuckling before he took a sip of coffee. "Just as well there aren't any wells around here."

"We're already in one." Tim looked grave.

"What do you mean?"

Tim sighed heavily. "There are only two, maybe three labs in the world that could have created Nan Airs, right? And yet some lone wolf Chinese scientist creates a working version in his basement?"

Evan had to admit Tim had a point. Before, he'd been caught up with the idea of the brilliant individual scientist, yet no matter how clever Weng proved to be, putting something like this into practice took resources. "Weng showed us a 30-second clip of some guy using the Nan Airs. We don't even know if they're safe."

"Guy did look a little pale."

Evan leaned back in his chair, contemplative. "I don't know who Weng's working with, but if they'd test it in a public marathon, what's stopping them from using it themselves? Sports would be changed forever. Ruined."

"Some would argue that," Tim said. "Remember the Lance Armstrong scandal? Armstrong said in that Oprah Winfrey interview that doping was the same as filling up his bike's tires with air, same as putting water in his water bottle. It's how these people think—"

"A whatever-it-takes-to-win mentality," Dana said, walking into the room.

Evan straightened his back awkwardly, surprised to see her. It was becoming increasingly difficult to act normal around DARPA, as their relationship progressed. It was especially challenging given that Tim had almost passed out earlier while he'd been distracted around her. Dana never appeared conflicted, however. Poised, sure of herself. And, lately, she never failed to chime in on the current matter of "enhancement," openly expressing her disdain for those who had to "cheat to win." It didn't seem consistent with the ruthlessness with which she went after career and personal goals. She was someone who needed to win in her life, but who still somehow found it wrong that people cheated in sports.

Evan was reminded of a study that found that one-third of scientists admitted to engaging in questionable research practices over the previous three years. There was also research by the psychologist Richard Byre at the University of St. Andrews who speculated that humanity's ability to deceive was innate. Faced with the chance of success, a substantial number of people cheated.

"People will always cheat in sports," Tim said. "There's just too much at stake now."

"Not everyone cheats," Evan said. "Some people do the right thing."

"Sounds like that soccer game that cost you your career."

Nine

Aegean sea, Greece

The fifteen swimmers vied for position in a small patch of the Aegean Sea. They clumped together, it being too early for one of them to make a break for it. Evan spotted Tim on a paddleboard between strokes. Tim was holding cupped hands over his mouth, shouting encouraging words, though it was impossible to hear them clearly with the frenzy of activity in the water. Evan kicked his legs and snatched water in a freestyle swim stroke. The water churned from thrashing of limbs, and Evan was struck repeatedly. One swimmer ahead of him accidently kicked him in the nose, dislodging his goggles. Just as he readjusted them, another swimmer mistakenly steered into him, the man's arms crashing into Evan's side. Evan gulped a mouthful of water and then lifted his head, coughing deeply.

An hour into the swim, the athletes had spread out more and Evan saw the first of four steel buoys, placed every three miles along the route. He steered himself toward it and tried to lose himself in the activity. The trick to managing the mind-bendingly long distances in an ultra-race was to break things down into small, manageable parts. He was taught to forget about the fact that he would travel 700 miles, but rather focus on one mile, or even a hundred feet at a time. It was one of many psychological games Evan had learned from his trainer.

The Aegean would probably have looked beautiful under different circumstances. Homer wrote about the sea having a "wine-dark" color. Evan's goggles gave him a clear view into the sea's depths. Within the blackness was a haunting strip of sunlight emanating from nothing. It triggered a raw kind of fear, a primal reaction the sea's vastness and the unknowns lurking in the deep. Occasionally there would be signs of life—a leer fish would dart by, or a jelly fish would float lazily into Evan's field of view. Mediterranean jelly fish, commonly known as fried egg jellyfish, would sometimes float too close and sting Evan's wrist or ankle. They would also bunch up in front of him, making it difficult to see.

Two hours in, Evan passed the second buoy and knew he was near the front. He was swimming hard—perhaps too hard. Hopped up on adrenaline, it was a common mistake to race too aggressively at the start and use up precious energy needed later in the race. Evan didn't care; he wanted to make a statement early. He lifted his head and was pleased to see that he was in third place, only two swimmers ahead of him. The two swimmers were side-by-side, slicing through the sea in sync with textbook form. Luke and McKnight.

Evan swam harder. It was foolish to use energy so recklessly, but he didn't care. For the next twenty minutes, he swam all out, his mind laser-focused on the leaders. His technique was flawless—his stroke, breathing, and timing were perfect, just as Lucian had taught him.

He caught up to Luke, who had fallen behind McKnight.

Evan cut through the water, passing Luke on the right. Between strokes, Evan glanced at his brother's face and saw fury. But Evan churned on about a hundred feet from the third buoy. While he was gaining on McKnight, Evan's lungs were screaming, his arms and legs begging for a slower pace. He didn't listen and maintained his speed, closing in on McKnight.

Evan caught him, too.

Evan was surprised to see McKnight pause in the water as Evan approached. McKnight jerked his foot into Evan's jaw. The blow caused Evan to see stars; he stopped, shook his head, and saw McKnight reach the buoy. Evan swam harder than before. He felt like a machine, his arms cutting into the water like propellers. As he reached the buoy, he noticed something just below the surface.

A body was on top of Evan, pushing him under the water. The attack caught Evan off-guard, so he wasn't able to take a breath. He gulped a mouthful of sea water and gagged as McKnight forced him below the surface. Panic overtook Evan and he thrashed wildly, but McKnight kicked his legs and held him under. The buoy was large enough to shield them both from the boats.

Evan reached around McKnight's back and his fingers felt the string to his wetsuit. He yanked it downward and cold sea water poured into McKnight's suit. McKnight gasped and released Evan in a panic. As Evan rose to the surface frantically, McKnight tore Evan's goggles away. Evan didn't care; he needed air. He burst through the surface only to see Luke pass him. Evan looked back—McKnight was fumbling with his wetsuit. It wouldn't be long until he was swimming again, this time with anger behind each stroke.

* * *

McKnight had announced his race to the world on television. As the Chairman and President of the McKnight Charitable Trust, McKnight had been invited to fundraising events at DARPA, as the majority of the Trust's $2 billion in assets went to cutting-edge medical research. McKnight was so taken by the *Excelsior* program during his visit that he made a $750 million donation to make Nan Airs a reality.

On television, McKnight exuded an undeniable charm across from the female journalist who was delivering a long introduction of the accomplished man. Evan had seen McKnight on similar interviews with Chris Matthews, Larry King, and even Oprah. He looked crisp in his black North Face fleece, jeans, and orange-laced Nike running shoes, an outfit that supported his "adventurer" brand, a completely different sentiment from the "financier" look he adopted in New York City, where he was also CEO and Portfolio Manager of Blackrock Capital Management.

Jack McKnight lived a double-life. One life was as prominent investor, a product of endless grooming from an early age—Philips Exeter to Princeton, then Harvard Business School and Wall Street. The second as a leader of harrowing and record-setting expeditions up mountains and cliff faces, across continents, and down unexplored rivers. As a mountaineer and rock climber, he was responsible for numerous first accents in the Himalayas and Yosemite

Valley. He set the speed climbing record up the Nose route of El Capitan at 1 hour and 43 minutes. *National Geographic* called him one of "the new breed of 21ˢᵗ century explorers."

McKnight was in his New York office for the interview that night, at a sturdy mahogany desk and a library behind him. The skin on his face was tough, weathered from exposure to environmental assaults over the years. He had escaped death several times in his adventuring, and had suffered many injuries. He nearly lost four fingers to frostbite on Everest, suffered a heart attack while climbing the Eiger in Switzerland, and spent two weeks in a coma after falling 30 feet while rock climbing in Yosemite. He also regularly competed in Ironman triathlons.

The reporter was fit and wore a tight black dress. "Mr. McKnight, always a pleasure."

McKnight shot the woman a winning smile. "Thank you." His voice was deep, laced with the kind of gravitas executive leaders possess, an intonation that captivated staff and wooed board members.

"Why don't you tell us why you're here?"

"By the time your show airs, I will have finalized plans for the most epic endurance competition ever imagined."

The reporter glanced at her notepad. "A triathlon, yes?"

"An *ultra*-triathlon."

"And that's swim, bike, run, right?"

"That's correct."

"What distances are we talking about, Mr. McKnight?"

McKnight looked pleased with himself. "A typical Ironman triathlon is a 1.2 mile smile, 112 mile bike ride, and—"

"A marathon to top it all off," the reporter said, obviously having done her research.

McKnight nodded. "I decided to multiply those distances."

"By what factor?"

"Five."

The reporter looked astonished. "For what purpose?"

McKnight was bold, unflinching. "To find out who's the best."

"The best of what?"

McKnight laughed. "The best athlete in the world."

McKnight's sense of self-importance knew no boundaries. The man was a megalomaniac, and a privileged member of the aristocratic class, who worked tirelessly to preserve his elite status in the world, endlessly searching for ways of benefiting a fortunate few over a disadvantaged many. Evan didn't find McKnight's donations to the *Excelsior* program generous. What sacrifice had he made by emailing his accountant to move a small fraction of his enormous wealth into a different account? McKnight was more than a self-important jerk, though. He was a tyrant who would bulldoze over anyone in the way of his goals. Evan couldn't help but wonder how many people McKnight had destroyed on his climb to the top of the financial and athletic world.

The reporter leaned toward a coffee table and retrieved a calculator. She typed, and her eyes widened. "So, that's a 12-mile swim, a 560-mile bike ride, and a 131-mile run. That must make it one of the longest races in the world."

"There are longer," McKnight said. "But the distance isn't all of it. The choice of route is everything. This route will be unforgiving."

"What is the name of the race?"

"It's called The Aletheia Ultratriathlon. 'The *Aletheia*' for short."

"Why *Aletheia*?"

"It's Greek for 'the state of not being hidden.' A 700-mile race should have the effect of revealing one's true self, I think."

"Can you describe the route?"

"The race begins on a barren peninsula in Faros, Greece, about sixty miles from Thessaloniki, the second-largest city in Greece. The athletes will leave the beach and swim 12 miles across the Aegean Sea to Kitros Salt Pit. From there, they will bike 560 miles to Sparta, passing Mount Olympus and traveling through punishing Greek terrain. They will then run 131 miles from Sparta to Egaleo Mountain. The winner will ride by way of chariot from Egaleo Mountain to Athens."

"And your race overlaps with the start of the Olympic Games, held in Athens this year?"

"As one ends, another begins," McKnight quipped. "The Aletheia and the games are intimately connected, yes. The winner should be crossing the finish line near the conclusion of the opening ceremony in the Olympic Stadium of Athens, known as 'Spiros Louis Stadium,' named after the first modern Olympic marathon race winner in 1896."

"And I understand the winner will have a special honor?"

McKnight looked particularly pleased with himself. "I have spoken to the Olympic organizing committee."

Probably meaning that he had bribed them. Or at least agreed to sponsor large portions of their operating costs.

"The champion will be the final bearer of the Olympic torch. This person will run toward the cauldron, up the staircase, and ignite the Olympic flame to officially start the Games."

The reporter shuffled her papers, bringing her notes to the top. "We asked scientific experts to review your race. Do you mind if I read a report from an exercise physiologist from the University of Pennsylvania?"

"By all means," McKnight said, looking unintimidated by the reporter's incredulous tone.

"This is what the head of UPenn's physiology department said, and I quote, 'this race, which is comprised of almost laughable distances through impossible terrain, is not only beyond the limits of human physiology, in terms of demands on the metabolic, cardiovascular, and skeletal systems, but will likely prove to destroy the bodies of all those who would attempt to complete it. Should a racer finish one leg, they will have accomplished something. To complete two, would be remarkable. In my expert scientific opinion, to finish this race in its entirety is not humanly possible, and trying to do so might well be characterized as an act of lunacy.'"

McKnight let out a deep belly laugh. Then he composed himself, and stared back unfazed.

The reporter squinted. "What do you say to an exercise scientist who believes the Aletheia is *impossible*?"

McKnight pulled back the sleeves to his fleece. "They will have to revise their opinions after the race." He adopted an almost aristocratic manner. "In

1954, in track and field, it was considered '*impossible*' for a human being to run a mile in under four minutes. Medical experts said that such a pace would cause the human heart to explode. But a runner named Roger Banister thought otherwise. When he ran a mile in 3:59:04, he changed what was considered possible in the sport. Today, the record is 3:43:13, a full 16 seconds faster than what medical science declared was humanly possible."

"What do you say to viewers at home who just don't understand why you would try and do such a thing?"

"If you have to ask what drives someone like me, you'll probably never understand." "Why Greece?"

"Because it's where sport originated." There was a bracelet on McKnight's arm, a chiseled warrior in body armor, thrusting a spear. "This is Achilles. He was an archetypal hero, the ideal achiever. Legend has it that Achilles was given the choice to live a quiet and long life, or a short and glorious one. He chose glory. There are those who will understand that. The few who are different from the rest. Those are the ones this race is aimed at."

The reporter tilted her head to one side. "And how many entrants do you have so far?"

"We have 14 participants already registered."

The reporter still looked like she had a bomb to drop. "And what do you make of allegations that some of your registered participants have tested positive for performance-enhancing drugs earlier in their careers?"

"I'm sure you're aware that it's an arms race between those who supplement illegally and the scientists who develop tests to detect them. But our athletes will be tested like any other sanctioned race. All of our registered athletes will be subject to random testing by the US anti-doping agency, and when they arrive in Greece, they will be tested by WADA officials."

"And what about new, more advanced technologies, such as those based on nanotechnology?"

For the first time in the interview, McKnight appeared uncool, seemingly unprepared for the question. "I know very little about this technology, though it's my understanding that such technology is theoretical, and technically impossible to create. I don't know the exact details of the anti-doping agency's testing strategies. Rest assured, if someone wants to cheat, they will be found and eliminated from competition."

The reporter hammered away. "Let's talk about the enormous cost of the race."

McKnight chuckled. "If there's anything I like talking about less than performance enhancement, it's the cost of my expeditions and races."

"I bring it up, because the race is estimated to cost around $6.5 million."

"If the accountants say so."

"Surely the accountants told you most of the race's expenses are coming out of your pocket."

McKnight was graceful. "I will be shouldering much of the financial burden for the race, yes."

"I wonder if you might comment on a recent favorable court ruling on your company, Blackrock Capital Management—one of the largest active fixed income investment management firms in the world."

"I'm not sure why we're talking about this," McKnight said, frowning, "but yes, a competitor of ours dragged us into court last year. And we won fairly, I might add."

"And yet many argue you won because the prosecutor couldn't locate an important document, a piece you weren't required by law to disclose, but for all intents and purposes should have submitted."

McKnight reacted as if he'd handled the question many times before. "I believe the relevant words there are 'weren't required by law.' I wasn't eager to go out of my way to provide documents that would cost my company millions, perhaps billions, of dollars."

The reporter looked displeased, but seemed to have tired of her hardline approach. "So, let's get back to the Aletheia. Tell me about those who have already registered. Any notables?"

"Greece's hometown favorite is Julius Leventis, a twelve-time winner of the *Ironman* triathlon in Kona, Hawaii. A reporter once asked him the same question you asked me: whether his pursuits were 'impossible.' He quoted Nietzsche: 'I know of no better aim of life than that of perishing in pursuit of the great and the impossible.'"

"Sounds like your kind of guy."

McKnight smiled. "Can't wait to meet him."

"There's also a 27-year-old Spanish rock climber turned endurance athlete named Isabella Dawson, right?"

McKnight nodded. "We also just registered a Harvard psychologist." His face brightened. "One of our first registrants was an up-and-comer in the world of endurance sports… Luke Galloway."

The name had been enough to stun Evan. Even so, the next words had burned through him.

"There is still one spot open," McKnight said. "When registration closes tomorrow, athletes will have a full year to train."

* * *

Evan found it hard to swim without goggles. The salt water stung his eyes, and he couldn't see clearly through the depths as he had been able to before his confrontation with McKnight. Somehow he managed to go the next three miles without them, opening his eyes every four or six strokes to make sure his path was straight. His eyes felt red and angry even with that precaution. He wanted nothing more but to stop and rub them, to try and relieve the pain. But doing that would have let the others get close to him. Would have squandered his hard-earned advantage. Instead of stopping, he kept his blistering pace, one stroke after another, making sure that McKnight couldn't catch up. As Evan passed the fourth buoy, he saw Luke thrashing his arms in distress.

Evan saw the problem. Luke was stripping jelly fish from his arms and shoulders. He had swum into a swarm of them. As Evan neared, Luke recovered and began swimming again. Evan swam up alongside him and the two cut through the water next to each other. The sea floor suddenly became visible, revealing a magnificent coral reef. Colorful sea creatures darted into holes and rocks as Evan and his brother bulldozed through the water above.

They stayed neck-and-neck for ten minutes. The shore was visible now, perhaps a mile away. Evan craned his neck back and saw McKnight nipping at their heels. Another athlete was also close, but couldn't see who it was. Evan had maintained a crazy pace, and the reckless use of energy started to catch up with him. His arms and legs felt heavy. Luke slowly inched away, a few feet at first; then ten, fifteen, a hundred. He realized then that Luke was stronger than him. Evan couldn't help a note of pride at that. His brother had come a long way. Evan had had his successes. Maybe it was time for his brother to have the spotlight.

Evan glanced behind him and saw trouble—the athlete in fourth place was floating on the surface of the water, bobbing on his back. McKnight swam past the suffering athlete, his wake flipping the person over, so that they floated face down. Luke reached the shore and jogged toward the first transition area. Evan shot a worried looked back at the athlete in trouble, unsure of what to do. McKnight was coming at him like a freight train. Evan made a decision; he did a 180 and swam toward the hapless swimmer. McKnight darted to the side, looking astonished, as Evan swam past him in the wrong direction.

Evan reached the swimmer. It was a big man with a thick jaw. He flipped him over and saw Julius Leventis, Greece's hometown hero. Julius was a specimen and the heart and soul of Greece, according to a major Athenian newspaper. A potter by trade, Julius lived an ascetic lifestyle in Dion, Greece, a small town about a quarter of the way into the race's cycling portion.

Julius's wetsuit was shredded across the chest, and blood trickled from a hundred tiny puncture wounds. He had swum too close to the reef.

Evan righted Julius in the water. "Can you hear me?"

Julius didn't answer. Evan placed his ear on the man's chest and felt a heartbeat. He was alive. He began beating the man's chest with his fist… once…. twice…

Julius coughed wildly while Evan kept his head above the water. Julius ejected mouthfuls of sea water in distress, and stuttered, "That… that… he ran me into the reef!"

McKnight hadn't played fair with Julius either, apparently.

"I can tow you," Evan said. "It's only a few hundred feet."

Julius murmured a jumbled phrase, but nodded weakly. Evan dragged Julius through the water as he moaned about the salt water splashing over his

mangled chest. They were moving at a snail's pace and other athletes caught up. McKnight was no longer in the water, likely through transition and on his bike.

From a competitive standpoint, helping Julius was unwise. Julius knew, too. "You should go, please," he said. "The others are catching up."

"I'm not going to let you drown."

One after another, athletes passed Evan and Julius, including Isabella. Evan had little chance to win at the start of the race. Now it was impossible.

Ten

Soccer used to be a kind of religion for Evan, the beautiful game. As Evan approached the soccer field at Alexandria High School, his head swimming from seeing Dana in bed with McKnight the night before, he heard a whistle and watched the players run toward the bench. It was early morning, and mist swirled around the soccer players' legs as they darted up and down the field. A young soccer player kicked the ball into the upper right-hand corner, curving it just out of the goalkeeper's reach. Evan remembered the feeling of a goal well. That small moment of triumph, supposedly one of the least common scoring moments in sport. Even baseball home runs were more common. Hearing the whistle brought back memories of hard soccer practices at the University of Oregon. He had been a star striker then. He smiled warmly as the kids surrounded their coach—*Evan's* old coach, Tom Helmsley. He'd been fired from Oregon shortly after Evan left.

Coach Helmsley was a compact, heavyset man with a balding head. His players huddled around him, breathing heavily from the drills. Evan sat down discretely on a bench close by, and watched Coach kneel down to address the players.

"C'mon," he said, "listen up." He pulled his broad shoulders back and scanned the group with a soft gaze. "As you know, my favorite coach was UCLA basketball coach John Wooden. Wooden never spoke about winning. After each game, he told his players to ask themselves one question: 'did you do the best that you were capable of?' He said that if you did the best you were

capable of, then the score didn't matter. But he also said if you did your best, he thought you will find the score to your liking."

It was Coach's favorite speech. Wooden told his players that they could focus on the outcome, but they shouldn't invest in it. "Invest, rather, in the process," he said. And not only will you have the satisfaction of having done your best, but you will probably find a favorable score as well.

Coach Helmsley stood up. "Alright guys, hands in." The players leaned in and stacked their hands on top of each other. Coach yelled, "*Process...* on three!"

The circle broke, and the players started collecting their gear.

Coach spun around and saw Evan. "Well, I'll be damned...the prodigal son returns. Man, how long's it been?"

"Not since..." Evan stopped short. The memory rushed back. It had been his senior year at the University of Oregon. In the school's most important game against Arizona State, in front of professional scouts, Evan had caught the ball during gameplay, because the goalkeeper had fallen.

With two minutes left in the game, Evan's team was on the attack. As the Arizona goalkeeper ran to corral the ball, he fell down injured. Evan's teammate should really have kicked the ball into touch to allow for treatment, but instead, he crossed the ball to Evan.

Instead of shooting on the unguarded net, Evan had caught the ball and informed the referee that the keeper was hurt. He was sent off for a deliberate handball. Evan's team lost the game in the penalty shootout that followed. A few weeks later, the school's administration let Coach go, and the professional scouts never gave Evan a second look.

"Still can't believe you caught that ball," Coach said, shaking his head in disbelief. "It was the best scoring opportunity we had all game."

Though fans had praised Evan for the act of sportsmanship, Evan had been devastated. His own players were in disbelief when it happened, as if he had made some horrible mistake. The act had alienated him from them. Evan regretted the decision immediately. He had never apologized to Coach for what happened, and thought perhaps it was as good a time as any. "Coach, I just wanted to say—"

"Don't say you're sorry."

"You lost the biggest game of your career because of me." Evan stuttered. "Professional scouts wouldn't touch me after that, and now you're coaching high school soccer."

Coach Helmsley shrugged. "Anyone else would have shot and scored in that moment." He scanned his players. "Any one of these kids would have." He pointed to one player, a scrawny boy skillfully juggling a ball for his friends. "That kid's the best player I have. Extraordinary technical skill and ball mastery; he's got college scouts on him like fleas on a dog. But he doesn't have moral bone in his body. These kids are growing up on reality TV, Ponzi schemes, and doping scandals. They believe they need to be ruthless and cut-throat to win."

Evan wasn't convinced. "You think what I did sent some kind of message?"

"Damn right it did." Coach watched players leave the field. "If only I could get these kids to listen. You did the right thing that day. And it won't be forgotten."

Evan picked up a soccer ball. He dropped it to his foot and juggled it skillfully. "Maybe you're right." He let the ball fall to the ground, and kicked it to the side.

"You're damn right, I am." Coach wrapped an arm around Evan's back. "So I was watching the news last night." He cleared his throat. "You think Luke might have bitten off more than he can chew with this ultra-triathlon?"

Evan was glad Coach brought that up. It was, after all, why he had visited him. "That's why I'm here."

"You wanted to talk about Luke's impulsivity?"

"I wanted to talk about mine."

"You're the least impulsive person I know—"

"I signed up for *The Aletheia*."

Coach let out a monstrous laugh. When he saw the look on Evan's face, he became serious. "You're joking."

"Before our dad died, he asked me to keep an eye on Luke, to make sure he didn't get into any more trouble. I should be there in case things go wrong." It was, of course, more than that, but there were things he wasn't about to tell his old coach.

"Look, you were a talented soccer player, best I ever coached. But soccer and triathlons are *totally* different sports. You're not an endurance athlete."

"I was hoping you could help me with that."

"So I guess you're looking for the stuff we used back in the day."

There was a reason Evan had caught the ball. It wasn't just about sportsmanship. It was about trying to make up for everything he and his team had already done wrong. Coach used to say things like, "it's not wrong, because everyone is doing it."

Indeed, everyone *was* doing it; Evan had just become the best of those that used performance enhancers. But supplementing slowly ate away at him and it rubbed off on people, his brother in particular. After Evan started using, Luke wasn't far behind. It was a temporary thing for Evan, but it led to addiction for Luke, and self-destruction. As Evan watched his brother decline, Evan told Coach that he was done using. He'd caught the ball two days later.

"I can't help you, Evan," Coach said. "I don't do that anymore. What you did… it reminded me that I had a choice."

"I don't want to do it that way either." Evan's tone was resolute. "I won't."

Coach thought for a moment. "There is a guy who might be able to train you… last name's Atticus. This washed-up dude from Greece who came to live over here. Rumor has it he doped his entire career and wrecked his body. He went clean, except for the booze, of course."

"Does he train athletes?"

"He's trained a few guys over the years, but gave it up. He's a total hermit now, living in this place on an olive grove."

"Where?"

"Up near Mather Gorge on the border of Maryland and Virginia."

"Mather Gorge, huh?" Evan walked away in earnest. "Thanks, Coach."

Eleven

Eastern Greece

Evan hauled Julius onto the shore and dropped him with relief. Julius pressed his face into the sand. Evan stood over him, breathing hard. Julius flipped onto his back, and clutched his wounded chest. He looked up to Evan. "Thank you."

Evan was breathing too heavily to answer. He pulled the zipper to his wetsuit and peeled it down to his waist. "Good luck."

Evan ran up the beach. Behind him, Julius called out. "American…"

Evan looked back.

"You are a good man."

Evan ran to the changeover area where volunteers were waiting. "Julius is back on the beach," he said. "He needs medical attention."

"We know," one of the volunteers replied. "Ms. Dawson told us."

Evan set about stripping out of his wetsuit. It came off smoothly and Evan was thankful for the lubricant he had applied earlier. He stuffed the wetsuit into the plastic box set out for it, careful to make sure it was all in there. He didn't think this race was one where competitors would really be disqualified for forgetting, but he didn't want to take the chance.

Underneath the wetsuit Evan wore a Zoot Ultra Tri Race Suit, an ultra-tight outfit which would support body temperature regulation as well as make him more aerodynamic on the bike. He jogged into an outdoor shower and washed the salty water off him, taking great care to spray his eyes, which still burned from the sea water. He ran on, into a narrow chute leading to the transition area. Hundreds of people shouted, blew horns, rang cowbells, snapped pictures, and waved signs with athletes' names on them.

Julius had a cult-following. As he lumbered to the medical tent, a swarm of fans followed behind a fence, crying "You can do it!" and "I love you, Julius!" McKnight had a respectable fan base as well. An American woman held a sign with McKnight's face on the cover of *National Geographic*. It was too typical that a man like McKnight was the pride of America, a man addicted to greed and power, who had spent his adult life preoccupied with making obscene amounts of money as a financier, and somehow thinking he had done something brilliant to deserve it. Evan wondered what McKnight's groupies might think if they knew who he really was. Would it make a difference to them?

There were seven bikes still left in the transition area, which meant half of the athletes had already started cycling. Evan spotted his *Specialized* road bike, one of the most aerodynamic models on the market. Even the hydration system was built into the frame to reduce crosswind drag. Evan stepped into his bike shoes and put on his *Uvex* helmet. Just as he grabbed the back seat of his bike, he noticed his back tire was flat. Tires occasionally popped from being pumped with too much air, but this time he knew that wasn't the case—someone had tampered with it. McKnight was taking no chances. On a modern racing bike, wheels were snapped in, but it would still take time.

Tim unexpectedly grabbed the bike from Evan's hands. "I'll switch this wheel out," he said. "Get something to eat."

Evan was glad to see his friend, and starving from the ten-hour swim. He rummaged through his duffel bag and found a treasure trove of food, which included dried cherries, bananas, energy gels, and Greek yogurt. While he ate, Tim made quick work of the repair. They both moved with urgency, knowing it was important to get through the transition area as fast as possible.

"There's green tea in a bottle over there," Tim said.

Evan finished a banana, and washed it down with the tea. He then shoveled Greek yogurt into his mouth frantically. Calories were vital now. Every mouthful was fuel.

"Four athletes dropped out during the swim," Tim said. "Only eleven left now." Tim fixed the new wheel into place. "There. You're good-to-go."

"You're the man, Tim."

"Aw, shucks." Tim handed Evan an undersized backpack. "It has regular water in one compartment, and coconut water in the other. There are energy bars and Gu packets in the pockets."

Evan mounted the bike. "See you at the half-way point."

Twelve

Arlington, Virginia

DARPA's Human Performance Laboratory was packed with scientists and uniformed officers from the Pentagon. Evan locked eyes with Weng. He was busy talking with DARPA's Director of public relations, a blonde bombshell who seemed to be designed to go in front of a camera somewhere. She was also a good liar, who seemed to be able to spin any story to the organization's advantage.

Judging by the glow on Weng's face, it was obvious he was ready for his fifteen minutes of fame. As Evan passed the two, he heard the woman say, "This is a big moment for you, Dr. Weng."

Evan squeezed through a group of men in suits. Then he saw Dana. She was dressed in her classic "innovator in chief" attire—a tight black sports coat and designer jeans. She was entertaining lieutenant general Edwin Somervell, the liaison between the Pentagon and the *Excelsior* program. The decorated three-star general had once been the Director of the Central Intelligence Agency and had 35 years in the United States Army. Now his role was keeping an eye on the things they came up with in the laboratories.

At least, when Dana allowed it. Dana always rolled out the red carpet for Somervell and his entourage, the attention obviously designed as a distraction. Just the way the game was played when it came to funding. Somervell relished the pampering, but he wanted results. Dana looked to be in good spirits, as she finally had some progress to report, thanks to Dr. Weng.

After seeing Dana and McKnight together the night before, Evan found Dana's entertainment style especially revolting. It was clear she would do anything to see her plans materialize, which included sleeping with *Excelsior's* greatest source of philanthropic funding. McKnight was standing at the center of a circle of admirers, fielding questions with his chest puffed out.

The same rage Evan had felt the night before bubbled up again. He wanted to walk up to McKnight and elbow him in the nose. The act would, of course, end his career at DARPA, but who cared? The government already had their breakthrough technology.

Evan saw Weng whisper in McKnight's ear, interrupting his conversation. McKnight brushed Weng away with his hand. How did they even know each other? He found himself hating both—Weng and his addiction to fame, McKnight and his obsession with personal glory. Two peas in a pod.

Evan spotted Tim glued to the wall at the back of the room. "You look like hell," Tim said, as Evan took a spot next to him. "Rough night?"

"You could say that." Evan wasn't going to admit that he had caught Dana cheating on him; he hadn't even told Tim that they were together. "You look nervous."

Tim's eyes shifted anxiously. "Too crowded in here. You should be the nervous one. Dana should be calling you up for a public service announcement anytime—"

"I think we can go ahead and get started," Dana said in a pleasant tone that still carried over all the conversations going on around her. She walked to the front of the room. "Thank you all for coming."

Tim nudged Evan. "After this, I need to show you something."

"What?"

"I made a little discovery last night."

Dana was still speaking. "The military has had a long-standing interest in improving its soldiers' performance on the battlefield. We can engineer perfect training regimens and nutrition programs. But there is little left to optimize. While there are always new exercises or dietary enhancements, the rate of performance improvement is flattening out. Many medical experts now believe that the outer limits of our athletic capacities have been reached." Dana paused, letting the implications of that sink in. Generals would always want their soldiers to be advancing, improving faster than any potential opposition.

"Since human performance has reached its limit, we must replace our own inefficiently designed systems."

Evan had heard the speech before. The rhetoric had originally been intended for Dana's keynote address to this year's annual meeting of the World Economic Forum (WEF), which brought together the world's most influential leaders from business, politics, and academia to discuss the most pressing issues of the day. The event normally took place in Davos, a mountain resort in the Eastern Alps, but this year it would happen in Washington, D.C., right in DARPA's backyard. The planning committee had asked Dana to deliver the opening speech, as the meeting's theme was focused on the legal use of performance-enhancing technology in sports and whether or not athletes should be permitted to use drugs in order to keep the progression of sports from stagnating.

Behind Dana was a white screen displaying an image of a human red blood cell. The cell was disk-shaped and biconcave. "No system needs upgrading more than the human red blood cell, the body's oxygen transporters. When oxygen is breathed into the lungs, it loads onto red blood cells. After these specialized cells are saturated with oxygen, they travel to distant tissues where oxygen is unloaded. Ninety-eight percent of oxygen-carrying sites on red blood cells are saturated at the lungs. At the tissues, saturation levels drop to 32%, which means only 66% of oxygen binding sites contribute to oxygen transport."

A new picture appeared on the screen, a man on the jacket of a book entitled, *Nanomedicine*. "In 1998, Tom Frietas wrote Nanomedicine, which detailed the designs for an artificial red blood cell with the capacity to deliver 2,366 times more oxygen per unit volume than red cells. He called them respirocytes." Dana searched the crowd. "To talk about respirocytes in detail, I'd like to invite up our expert scientist, without whom the *Excelsior* program would not be possible."

Evan stepped forward, nudging his way past a small group.

"Dr. Weng," Dana said, smiling at the Chinese scientist. "Would you care to join me?"

Evan stopped short. *Dr. Weng?* He trembled with barely contained fury as Weng proudly shook hands with Dana, and then faced the group. "Thank you for letting me speak today, Dr. Brines. As you can imagine, it has been an exciting few days, having solved DARPA's Grand Challenge. I'd like to thank Dr. Brines for opening her project up to the world. I'd also like to thank Mr. McKnight, as I understand that the McKnight Charitable Trust supported this innovative challenge." On the screen was a new image, a spherical-shaped respirocyte. "This is an artist's rendition of a respirocyte, which I call a Nan Air."

Evan couldn't believe it. The name "Nan Air" had been *his* idea.

Weng continued, "These nanodevices were only theoretical until I created the precise calculations to make the mechanics work. As you can see here, the pressure vessel is spherical in shape. Inside is a nanometer-sized onboard computer with chemical sensors, which monitor the partial pressure differences at the lungs and the tissues. Just as hemoglobin does inside red blood cells, these sensors know precisely when to pick up oxygen or release it."

Dana stepped forward. "Today, you will see three demonstrations that will prove, first-hand, the extraordinary power of Nan Airs." Dana led the audience to a treadmill. A man in his twenties stood next to it, dressed in a military uniform.

Dana patted the cadet on the shoulder. "Five minutes ago, we infused this young man's blood with Nan Airs." She gave the solider a nod. "Please step onto the treadmill." He stepped on, and technicians attached a facemask to his head. Wires and tubes fed back to a desktop computer on a wheeled cart. The technician pressed some buttons on the treadmill, and the cadet began jogging. Dana turned the computer monitor toward the group and pointed to the number, seventy-eight. "Here, we're monitoring maximum rate of oxygen consumption, known as VO2max. In exercise physiology, VO2max is a common measure of aerobic fitness. The average untrained male has a VO2max of about 45 ml/min/kg."

General Somervell stood by the machine. "What about highly trained endurance athletes, like in cycling or cross-country skiing?"

Evan elbowed his way to the front. "World-class athletes typically achieve scores in 80s, occasionally breaking into the low 90s."

Dana didn't look pleased with the interruption, but she stayed professional. "Forgive me, General Somervell. I forgot to introduce you to our limit physiologist, Dr. Evan Galloway." She placed a hand on Evan's back. "I think I can take it from here, Dr. Galloway."

Somervell didn't seem to want to discard Evan so quickly. "So, what's the highest VO2max ever recorded, Dr. Galloway?"

"That would be 97.5 by Oskar Svendsen, an 18-year-old cyclist from Norway." Evan looked at the cadet's VO2max, and managed to maintain an air of scientific objectivity. "As you can see, Nan Airs have allowed this man to utilize oxygen *perfectly*."

"He's not even breathing heavily."

Dana smiled at that. "We made the inefficient circulatory system 100% efficient. Watch this." She leaned in close to the solider. "Cadet, please hold your breath."

The young man took a deep breath and continued running. Dana nodded at the technician who increased the treadmill's speed from five miles-per-hour to six. The soldier skipped into a jog. The speed increased to seven miles-per-hour then eight. The cadet gave the thumbs up for more speed. He broke into a full sprint as the speed increased to thirteen miles-per-hour. All while holding his breath.

"Unbelievable," Somervell said. "How long do the Nan Airs last?"

"White blood cells clear them from circulation after about four days."

"And then you need another injection?"

"Correct," Dana said. "Now if I can escort you to the next demonstration." The group walked to a large sphere, maybe ten feet in diameter, filled with water. Floating eerily at the bottom was a man in swim shorts, staring blankly at the crowd of observers. Dana pointed to a technician on a ladder. "How long has this man been holding his breath?"

"Eighteen minutes."

The general looked astounded, along with everyone else. There were whispers and light chatter among the visitors.

"Eighteen minutes," Dana said. "When you or I could not hold ours for five. Gentlemen, the Nan Airs work. Now, why don't we continue the tour?"

She set off out of the room, leaving Evan behind.

Thirteen

The sun sat low in the sky, adding glare to the other conditions as Evan pedaled into strong headwinds. The course cut through the Kitros Salt Pit, a nondescript stretch of salt marshes that would have amplified the heat during the day but now seemed almost to leach it away. One crosswind almost tipped him over, so he had to sit low and stabilize the bike to avoid tipping over. He approached two athletes riding side-by-side, obviously pacing themselves, and he blew past them. He rode several miles along a quiet road running parallel to the Thessaloniki–Athens highway, and then took a sharp left turn onto the Macedonia road. Traffic wasn't a problem so far, but he was still cautious at each junction. It wasn't a closed course, the way it was for some events, and bikes were often hard to see.

Most ultra-triathletes at the elite level would finish a quintuple Ironman in about three days. Average competitors could take around four, five, or even six days. With Nan Airs, McKnight would finish in less than three. Evan had lost ground during the swim, so he had to make up time on the bike, and that wouldn't be easy. But then, nothing about the race was easy.

The bulk of the race was the cycling portion, a 560-mile ride across Central Greece and down the eastern coast to Sparta in the middle of the Peloponnese peninsula. Most of the athletes would bike through the night on the first day, because stopping to rest would mean being overtaken. When they reached the village of Paramythia, about 215 miles away, they might sleep for a few hours. If

Evan maintained a speed of approximately 35 miles per hour he could make it to Paramythia in perhaps eight and a half hours. Then it would be 310 miles to Sparta.

Evan had expended more energy than he would have liked during the swim, but the fresh sea air and spectacular views were invigorating. He did have to give McKnight one thing: he had chosen a marvelous place for his race. Evan rode down the eastern coastline for six miles, cutting through Mediterranean villages with endearing wood-framed houses, hotels, spas, and watering holes. He rode past cafés with outdoor seating, and got nods from patrons enjoying wine or espressos. The narrow streets were packed with spectators with cow bells and bull horns. Sometimes a brash adolescent would break from the crowd and sprint next to Evan for a few hundred feet before peeling off to catch their breath.

The street names were impossible to read, but the course was well-marked with signs, and volunteers stood at confusing intersections or roundabouts, waving flags to point athletes in the right direction. Evan passed another athlete around a sharp corner and was waved right by a volunteer toward Katerini, a small agricultural town and a popular tourist destination due to its proximity to the village of Dion and, of course, Mount Olympus, which was already visible in the distance.

Tim followed, of course. He was in a support car now, driving up close to Evan so that he could talk. "How are you doing, man?"

Evan squeezed in words between heavy breaths. "Good, good."

"Eight miles to Dion. There's a pretty steep downhill coming up."

Evan smiled at that. "I need to make up time."

Tim lifted a map to his face, driving with one hand. "It's about a 12% gradient, so you might want to take it easy."

Evan charged the downhill, and shifted his weight back on his seat. He held his body low, creating as aerodynamic a position as he could hold. As he picked up speed, the bike wobbled, but Evan gripped the handlebars tight as the warm air whipped across his face.

Tim yelled out speeds somewhere beside Evan. Evan didn't look around, because to do so would be to break from his position.

"60 miles per hour."

Evan pedaled harder.

"70 miles per hour."

Evan started to pull away.

"80!"

Evan's consciousness narrowed. All that mattered were the microscopic details that kept him upright.

He reached the bottom and saw the bike race's first casualty, a man sitting next to a mangled bike, blood dripping from his knees, elbows, and face. It looked like he had lost control and had steered into a wooden fence, too badly wounded to resume. Thankfully, it didn't appear that he'd suffered any seriously broken bones.

Evan pulled into Dion, a small city twenty-six miles from the beach at Kitros Salt Pit. Evan was satisfied with his fast pace, and thought perhaps he had put a dent in McKnight and Luke's commanding lead. He approached an aid station where volunteers stood along the road to pass out energy drinks and sugar-dense snacks like fruit, pretzels, gels, and granola bars. He could have stopped to enjoy something hardier like oatmeal or chicken broth, which would have helped replace the sodium he had lost from sweating, but it was 8:30 pm and he wanted to reach the heart of Dion before nightfall.

* * *

Evan's mind drifted back to DARPA as he rode. To the Pentagon visit. The shock of Dana's infidelity was still fresh then. Why had Dana slept with McKnight? Was it boredom with the relationship? He'd watched Dana laugh with General Somervell and then say goodbye like nothing was wrong. Did she even feel any sense of guilt about what she'd done?

Dana had tried to scoot past Evan unnoticed after the demonstrations to the Pentagon. But Evan snatched her elbow. "Are we going to talk about last night?"

Dana had daggers in her eyes. "Let go of my arm."

"I can't believe you slept with that narcissistic piece of garbage."

Dana composed herself. "Let's talk in my office."

Evan wanted to say yes, but then he saw Tim. He'd needed to talk to him. And maybe it would be good to give himself some time to cool off, too.

"Five minutes," Evan said, heading for Tim.

He didn't get there, though. As Evan approached Tim, he felt a firm hand on his shoulder.

"What's up, bro?"

Evan spun around to see his brother, flustered and out of breath.

"What are you doing here?" Evan said. Evan wanted to focus on his brother, but he was distracted by Dana who had interrupted McKnight's conversation with one of the prettier female technicians. The technician looked like she wanted to run.

Tim joined Evan and Luke, looking to Evan's brother. "Do you have a visitor's pass?"

"Take a hike, four eyes," Luke said.

Tim meandered away, a "wish-I-was-invisible" expression on his face.

Luke turned to Evan. "I just looked at the *Aletheia's* registration list. What are you doing on it?"

Evan watched Dana over Luke's shoulder. "Look, Luke, it's complicated."

Luke stepped into Evan's line of sight again. "That's a load of crap. You just couldn't help yourself, could you? I was getting good at something, and you just couldn't let me be the best."

"That's not true."

It was about protecting Luke, not about beating him. And it was about McKnight. It was about beating *National Geographic's* cover boy in his own race.

Luke didn't look like he believed it. "So why did you register? You're a soccer player, not a triathlete. A *former* soccer player."

Evan couldn't tell him the truth. Luke wouldn't want to hear that Evan was trying to look out for him. Saying it hadn't worked before, had it?

"Maybe I'm out of shape and I want to prove something," he tried. It was a weak lie, and it didn't do anything to placate Luke.

"If you're out of shape, sign up for a 5K or a sprint triathlon—*not* a quintuple ultra-triathlon." Luke looked inquisitive. "Wait a minute… is this about when you choked? Are you trying to redeem yourself for not scoring or something?"

Evan wasn't listening by then. He watched McKnight whisper something to Dana. She threw her head back and laughed. Evan clenched his teeth, and stepped towards them. Maybe leaving it five minutes to cool off hadn't been such a good idea after all. Luke grabbed his arm before he could walk over though, with such force it spun him around, eye-to-eye.

"Don't walk away from me," Luke said.

"Luke, I need—"

"And what *you* need is always more important than what I need, isn't it? Well, you'd better train hard this year, man. This is 700 miles of competitive racing, not some pick-up game of soccer. When we get to Greece, we're not brothers; we're competitors."

He stormed away.

Evan stood there watching him go for a moment or two. He'd known all his life that Luke tried to outdo him where he could, but this was something different. If it had been any other time, he would have gone after his brother and tried to explain himself. Instead, the moment just fueled the anger inside him. Evan marched across the room like a freight train, barging into the middle of McKnight and Dana's conversation. He raised his finger in McKnight's face, but, like the night before, couldn't find the words.

McKnight grinned. "Cat got your tongue, big guy?"

Evan made a fist with his hand. He thought about swinging at him, but steadied himself.

Dana stepped between them. "I think it's time for that meeting, Evan."

Evan turned to walk away. McKnight didn't let him. "You know I saw that little soccer game of yours. I know the scouts didn't give you a second look after your team lost. Still, at least you can feel good about doing the right thing. A professional career isn't really *that* big of a deal."

Even Dana seemed unhappy with that. "Jack, leave him alone—"

Evan found the words this time. "You think you're some kind of hero, don't you? He pointed to McKnight's bracelet, the one he'd been showing off in the interviews. "You think if Achilles were alive today he would have gotten an MBA, and founded an investment firm? You're not a hero. You're just a suit with an army of attorneys."

McKnight didn't seem affected. "Tell me, where did catching that soccer ball get you? You lost, Galloway. You threw away what you wanted, when you could have snatched it with both hands. I won't apologize for what I do. I don't feel bad for being unsentimental. It's the only way to actually win in life."

"And that's the problem with hero myths," Evan said. "It's men like you telling the world that it has to be your way. It doesn't have to be."

McKnight just smiled at that. "Prove it."

Fourteen

Dion, Greece

Almost 200 miles into the cycling section, Julius pedaled up alongside Evan. Evan was glad to see that he had recovered, even though it was slightly frightening that the big Greek had managed to make up so much ground on him.

Without slowing, Julius held out a banana to Evan. Evan accepted the gesture gratefully. As Evan ate, his eyes were drawn to the looming shape of Mount Olympus, its snow-covered tip cloaked in mist and low clouds.

"It's beautiful to ride up," Julius said beside him. "Plus it gives people plenty to gossip about when it comes to training."

Evan had read some of the articles that talked about Julius "training with the gods." He'd cycled through the Olympus mountain range with a backpack full of stones, performing training runs up the highest mountain in Greece.

Evan looked over at the other man. "You're from Dion, right?"

Julius nodded and threw the peel from his banana to the side of the road. "The city of Dion was built to honor Zeus and the other gods of Ancient Greece."

"It's a holy city, then."

"I believe a race like this is too difficult for a human to complete alone. The Gods must help us." Julius didn't pull his eyes away from Mount Olympus.

Evan wasn't religious, but he couldn't deny that there was something spiritual about the place. It had an old-world feeling—the rugged terrain, meadows with tall cedars and black pines, the lush ravines and craggy hilltops. He could hear the faint clicking of hooves as a man led a mule down a cobblestone path.

Julius smiled as he rode. "Smell the fresh air, see the clean water. It is unspoiled. It's *pure*."

Julius was right. Things seemed so natural and organic. Julius seemed to personify the spirit of the setting. Unlike others in the race—McKnight, even his own brother—Julius seemed pure. Evan felt a kindred spirit at his side.

The sun sunk below the horizon, and Mount Olympus became cloaked in darkness. Evan clicked on his headlamp and the flashlight mounted on his handlebars. Julius did the same, and the two biked silently in the fading light.

Fifteen

Arlington, Virginia
DARPA

Dana sat down at her desk, opened a drawer, and pulled out a small-framed picture of Michael McKnight—Jack's son. *Her* son. She wiped away a smudge with her thumb and felt the tears well up. It had been hard for her not to burst into tears as Weng showed them the video of the Great Wall marathon. She'd known Michael had it in him to be a great man, even though she hadn't spent time with him since he was a child.

At least, he would have been great if McKnight hadn't cut his life short. She used to watch Michael's high school track meets—from afar, of course. She always kept her distance, having made the decision a long time ago to stay out of his life. There was a bust of Achilles on Dana's desk, a gift from McKnight. A part of Dana wanted to smash it into fragments. It was only there at all because McKnight liked to lay claim to the people around him with gifts.

Evan walked into her office, and she scurried to get the picture back into the drawer. After thinking about Michael, it occurred to her that she must appear softer than usual, not the image of a hardened executive that she always had to present to the DARPA staff. Such an image was simply necessary in today's world, especially for a woman at the highest levels. You had to harden yourself into a hammer to break through the glass ceiling.

"Have a seat, Evan." She circled behind him and closed the door.

How much did he know? He seemed tense. She knew he despised her after catching her cheating on him with McKnight. Amazing that a man could cheat with impunity, but when a woman did, it was done.

Evan sat down in a seat across from Dana. "Do you love him?"

She thought that was abrupt. But *no*, of course not, she thought. To her, McKnight was just as arrogant and self-obsessed as Evan thought. She lowered into her seat, and adopted a fake sincerity. "I think so."

"I know we didn't put any labels on anything," Evan said in a desperate tone, "but I thought we were, I don't know, a couple?"

"I didn't see this coming," Dana said softly. "Jack asked me to dinner when we were raising money for the *Excelsior* program. It was innocent at first. Just about catching up on the past. One thing led to another—"

"Until I catch you two together *the day* we figure out the Nan Airs?"

"Well, actually, Dr. Weng figured it out."

"Tim and I would have solved it." Evan shook his head. "Our calculations seemed spot on. I still can't believe we didn't—"

"That's why we're having this meeting, Evan." There was a knock on the door. A dark-haired woman was waiting to come in, holding a vanilla envelope. Dana waved her hand, gesturing the woman from Human Resources forward. "Come in."

She moved across the room with robotic precision, her gait exacting. "Evan, I'm Cynthia from—"

"HR." He leaned forward, and Dana could see how nervous he was. "Um, what's going on here?"

Cynthia crossed the room and took a seat beside Evan. "Evan, given Dr. Weng's discovery, Dr. Brines has officially discontinued the *Excelsior* program." She lifted the vanilla folder. "Now in this package of materials—"

Evan looked at Dana, not at Cynthia. She should have expected that. "You're firing me?"

Dana nodded to Cynthia, who pursed her lips. It was more professional if she did this. "Your employment with DARPA is being discontinued, yes. In order for you to collect employment insurance, both Dana and I have agreed the appropriate reason for termination will be 'poor performance.' I understand this will be a difficult transition, but—"

"Poor performance?" Evan stared at Dana. "That's ridiculous. I was *six months* into this research project, an agenda to create a technology that most scientists had dismissed as theoretically impossible." He paused. "Tim was right. He said you'd fire us when you got your prize."

Dana shook her head. "It's not like that, Evan."

"Then what is it like?" Evan demanded.

"The project is over. What did you expect to happen?"

Cynthia answered. "We've decided to keep Tim on board to manage the data transfers, but, as of this moment, the *Excelsior* program has been cancelled, and we will begin sending the 30-person lab home as of today." She rose from her seat. "I will see you out. I'll have to accompany you while you clean out your desk, and you won't be able to take any files with you."

Evan stared at Dana coldly. "You used me. You used all of us."

Dana said nothing, carefully adjusting documents on her desk. "You were never really cut out for the politics, Evan. And I haven't 'used' you. You've done a job. The job is done. Now you need to go. Please don't make this harder than it has to be. Security will be here in a moment."

Sure enough, Dana's office door opened to reveal a large man in a black suit. He laid a hand on Evan's back and nudged him out of his seat. "Let's go, young man."

Evan stood up and as he did so, his arm caught the bust of Achilles. It tumbled to the ground and split into several jagged pieces. "Oops."

Dana thought the act of defiance was amusing, even if it was also childish. She'd been thinking of doing the same just a little while ago. As Evan, Cynthia, and the security guard walked out of her office, she slid open her drawer and retrieved the picture of Michael. She brought it close to her face, matching her eyes with her son's. Then she drove the frame into the corner of her desk, shattering the glass. She pulled out the picture and tucked it into her pocket.

Sixteen

Central Greece

Evan and Julius traveled long stretches of rural roads together, the hum of their bikes disturbing tiny creatures in bushes, behind rocks. For the time being, it made sense. They were competitors, but there was also something like brotherhood between them as they rode. Julius' presence meant that the two of them could take turns drafting and saving energy, but it also broke up the solitary monotony of the ride.

Sometimes the terrain changed to dirt, which made the bikes hard to control with their skinny tires. Evan had about ten feet of visibility in front of him, even with the headlamp and flashlight. At a speed of 30 miles per hour, he would likely arrive at Paramythia before sunrise, perhaps around five in the morning After a few hours of riding side-by-side, Evan decided to split up with Julius, and rode hard to perhaps see if he could catch up with Luke. He broke clear and pushed until Julius was left well behind him, his lights only a faint glow in the dark.

His butt had started to ache from the rock-hard seat; it was just one of the many annoyances that had crept up during the grueling journey. His body had already started waging mini rebellions. His training as a physiologist helped him diagnose these pains and work out what he needed to do about them. Cramping, for example, simply meant he needed to replace electrolytes. Gatorade provided an ideal mix of sodium and potassium, the vital salts that supported digestion, nervous and cardiac function, as well as proper muscle contraction. In an ultra-endurance race like the *Aletheia*, maintaining physiological balances of fuel, electrolytes, and hydration was a constant battle.

Riding through the night calmed Evan's mind, and gave him time to muse. When Dana had fired him, Cynthia had hovered over his shoulder as he brushed notepads, pencils, and lab books from his desk into a cardboard box. He cringed as a small replica of Charles Darwin hit the bottom of the box with a thud. Scientists behind him were also packing up their belongings, whispering, quietly furious at the speed with which things had changed.

Just five months before, Evan had felt like he'd had a career rocket ship strapped to his back at DARPA, newly minted as the *Excelsior's* program leader. His project was well-funded and highly respected. Now it was just dead. And he was a disgrace. Maybe McKnight was right. Maybe achievement required his kind of cut-throat, Machiavellian tactics. Maybe cheating was rewarded, not fair play. And maybe Evan wasn't hard enough for the way the world worked.

Tim approached him then. He'd been right that Weng's discovery would make them obsolete. Tim looked more awkward than usual, as if he were having trouble playing it cool. Tim straightened his back matter-of-factly, and stuck out his hand. "It was a pleasure working with you, Dr. Galloway."

Evan guessed that it was a charade for Cynthia. "You, too."

They shook hands and Tim patted Evan on the back. This time he was sincere. "You're the best man I know." Then Tim lowered his voice to a whisper. "Meet you at your car, ten minutes."

Cynthia narrowed her eyes, but Tim's words were too soft to hear.

Ten minutes later, Evan was standing beside his black Volvo, tapping his keys against his leg anxiously. Scientists were spilling into the parking lot, holding their heads low. Sometimes Evan would exchange a look of defeat with a colleague, but everyone mostly kept to themselves. Evan swiveled his head across hundreds of employees' cars. There was no sign of Tim, and it made him anxious to wait when undoubtedly security was watching him through the cameras attached to the light posts overhead. He looked back at DARPA with contempt. Dana was probably watching him from her office, making sure he wouldn't do anything that might tarnish the reputation of the organization.

Evan glanced at his watch. He couldn't wait any longer. He unlocked his door and hopped into his car. He fiddled with his rearview mirror and then jerked his head back in shock; Tim was sitting quietly in the back of his car.

"You scared the hell out of me," Evan said.

"Listen, we don't have much time," Tim said, speaking rapidly. "I analyzed Weng's Nan-Air designs, and compared them with ours."

Evan didn't want to talk about the Nan Airs. "Look, man, I don't care."

"You should."

Evan paused at that. "Why?"

"Because the designs are the same as ours."

Evan spun around to face Tim. "That's right," Tim said, "There's no difference between the outsourced Nan Airs and ours."

"We had the correct design all along?"

"We actually figured it out in the first *three weeks*. I hacked into archived files on the server, and found our original data. Someone was manipulating it, making it seem like we hadn't solved the design."

"Dana." There was no one else who could have done it. Evan thought for a moment. "We issued the Grand Challenge a month into the *Excelsior* program, which means she had us outsource the project *after* we had already solved it?"

Tim nodded. "Makes no sense, right?"

"What would she want Weng to do?"

"Maybe to make modifications, or design another prototype. There's something else." Tim looked out his window nervously and then pulled out his iPhone. "Check this out." He pressed play on a video, and the two watched a runner sprint along what looked to be the Great Wall of China.

Evan's eyes narrowed. "The Great Wall Marathon?"

Tim bit his lip, and nodded.

"Is this the video Weng showed us?"

"No. This was uploaded to YouTube a few days ago by a Chinese reporter." Tim fast-forwarded the video toward the ending. "Watch this."

On the screen were two men helping a runner into a black suburban. With their backs to the camera, they disappeared inside the van. Tim advanced the video. The suburban's driver's side window lowered, and small puffs of smoke floated through the window. Tim asked, "Notice anything familiar?"

Evan shook his head. Then the man in the driver's seat rested his forearm on the door. On the man's forearm was a gold bracelet with black etchings. Evan only knew one man with a bracelet like that, a man who also liked to smoke cigars. *McKnight.* "McKnight is working with Weng?"

"Two points for you."

Evan saw two well-built security guards stride out of DARPA's main entrance. Things suddenly became intense. "We've got company."

Tim glanced at the guards and then spun around quickly. "There's one more thing."

Through his rearview mirror, Evan watched the guards scan the lot for his car. They didn't have much time. "Hurry up."

Tim unfolded a newspaper article, and handed it to Evan. The headline read: *Olympic distance runner suspended for doping.* Tim said, "The article's about a runner who got busted for doping before the Olympics."

A guard spotted Evan's car, and then skipped into a jog. Evan read the first paragraph frantically, and then summarized it for Tim. "Okay, so the anti-doping agency found out this guy was doping, and suspended him from the games... so what?"

Tim handed Evan another article. "Check this one out." Evan saw the article was dated a few days before from the *Shanghai Daily* website. The headline read "Winner of Great Wall Marathon found dead in Hai River." Dead? Evan read from the article aloud. "The autopsy report says the young white male showed signs of systemic immunological reaction likely caused by severe infection."

The guards were thirty feet away. Tim still wasn't done though. "Compare the names in the articles."

Evan scanned the first article and then sucked in a quick breath, as he kept reading. "The body was identified to be the winner of the Great Wall Marathon, Michael McKnight, son of American financier and billionaire, Jack McKnight. The runner delivered a commanding performance at the marathon, but left the finish line quickly. Later, his body was found in the Hai River."

The security guards surrounded the car on both sides. One knocked on Evan's window. Evan ignored them, and spoke fast to Tim. "McKnight used the Nan Airs on his *own son*?"

"And it killed him," Tim added.

"But our version of the respirocytes never did that. So why would Weng's do it, unless…" Evan swallowed at the implications of that thought. "Unless it was deliberate."

"Exactly," Tim said. "I think DARPA issued the Grand Challenge to create a weaponized version of respirocytes."

Evan didn't want to believe it, but it made sense. Part of Nan Air's appeal was that they could be triggered remotely to boost the body's performance as required. If they could also be lethal on demand, then DARPA had just created the ultimate poison. One that could stay in someone's system, and then kill them at a signal. It would create a way to kill someone precisely without obvious weapons and without the uncertainty of regular poisons. More than that, it would allow the military to control people with just the threat of activating the lethal version of the respirocytes. All that, and they still got the improved performance of the regular version.

The guards had reached the car now. One leaned down to eye level, speaking through the window. "Evan Galloway: you are now considered a trespasser. Leave the premises immediately, or we will be forced to detain you."

The other guard glared at Tim in the backseat. "Open the door now Tim or I'll break the window."

Tim leaned forward. "You think McKnight will use the Nan Airs in the triathlon?"

Evan nodded. "He'll use our version. The safe version."

Tim reached to unlock his car for the guards. "Evan, the article says McKnight's son won the marathon by an hour. How's anybody supposed to compete with someone supplementing with Nan Airs?"

Evan didn't have a good answer to that. "I guess I'd better find a good trainer."

Seventeen

Central Greece

Around one in the morning, Evan saw bright blue and red flashing lights several miles down the road. He made out a few police cars and ambulances. Volunteers waved flags to direct Evan around the center of the chaos.

"What happened?" Evan asked, pressing the front brake on his bike.

The nearest volunteer lowered his flag. "Accident at the intersection. Use the left shoulder to circle around."

Tim suddenly ran up behind the volunteer. He'd obviously driven ahead. "Evan. Jeez, man, I'm glad you're here."

Evan slowed to a stop. The lights from the cop cars were almost blinding. He saw a twenty-something lying flat on a stretcher with a neck brace. "What the hell's going on?"

"There was a big crash," Tim said. He was out of breath. "Four or five athletes were involved."

Evan felt a rush of worry. "Was Luke in it?"

Tim looked into the mess and bit his lip.

Evan's eyes widened. "Is he okay?"

Tim ran a hand through his hair. "I don't know. It was pretty bad."

Evan pedaled toward the carnage and saw mangled bikes and broken equipment strewn across the road. One woman was trying to repair her bikes with a wrench; another guy was tending to a bleeding knee. Then he saw Luke. He was dragging his damaged bike from the wreckage. The front tire on his bike was folded in half, and the frame had a massive crack down the middle. The back of his bike shirt was tattered and blood trickled from open gashes on his shoulder. He also had a large gash on his chin, which he didn't seem to care was gushing blood.

Evan leapt off of his bike and ran toward Luke. He tore off his shirt, balled it up, and pressed it against Luke's chin. Luke shoved Evan away. "Get away from me."

"Damn it, Luke, you're bleeding badly." Evan lifted the bloody shirt. "Will you just let me—?"

Luke pushed Evan harder this time, sending Evan backpedaling.

"Fine," Evan said. "You don't want my help, *fine*." Evan lifted his bike off the ground and threw a leg over the seat.

"That's right. I *don't* need your help. I can live my life perfectly fine without the watchful eye of my big brother."

Evan was ten feet away when he heard: "And I don't care what Dad thinks."

Evan stopped in his tracks. Their father hadn't come up in a long time.

Luke continued. "You think I don't know about your little pact with him? The one where you're supposed to watch over me, make sure I don't do anything stupid?"

"I just wanted to make sure—"

"You were always the family's high standard. And I could never live up, could I?" Luke's face turned sour as Evan looked back. "I've spent my whole life trying to catch up to you. Now *I'm* in the lead."

Evan stared at his brother for a few moments. "I'm proud of what you've accomplished. You got clean in rehab. You've won all these races."

Luke looked ashamed then.

Evan continued. "At first I didn't know how to deal with your success. I might have been a little jealous at first. But I'm not jealous; I'm proud of you."

"You shouldn't be proud of me."

"Why not?"

Luke pulled an object from a pocket and tossed it to the ground. "*This is why.*"

Evan watched a glass vial shatter across the pavement. Immediately he knew it was a vial of Nan Airs. He couldn't believe it. "How did you... how could you get access—?"

"How do you think I won all those ultra-races?"

He had been using the whole time.

"I met Jack McKnight in my first triathlon out of rehab. After the race, he approached me. Said I had potential, that I could be better. I had seen his success—the guy was a rock star. He gave me the first injection before The Western States 100-Mile Endurance Run. He came in first, I came in second."

Now Evan knew why Luke had been awkward around McKnight at DARPA. McKnight had been using Luke as a test subject, giving him access to the drugs almost from the start.

"How did you get access?"

"McKnight has history with Brines. It probably also helped that he was the biggest donor to support the *Excelsior* project."

"But what about rehab?"

"Turns out I wanted to win more than I wanted to stay sober." He lowered his head. "Just once I wanted to be better than you."

"But not this way, Luke."

"There you go with your morals, always so high and mighty. You act like you're squeaky clean, like you didn't use in college. You think McKnight gives a damn about fair play? You think any of the other athletes do?"

"I do!" Evan shouted back at him.

"That's right! Evan Galloway, ladies and gentlemen." Luke's outburst was loud enough that the crowd could here. "He can do anything he puts his mind to." Luke's eyes welled up with tears. "I was going to stop using them, you know. I was going to race without Nan Airs. When I heard you registered, I stayed on them."

"Why?"

"Because how else was I going to beat you?" He shook his head disbelievingly. "I honestly have no idea how you are even keeping up."

"Cut it out, and let's get back in this race."

"My bike's shot... I'm done."

Evan whistled loudly to Tim. "Hey!"

Tim appeared, always dependable. "What's up?"

Evan pointed to his brother. "Grab the spare bike for Luke."

"You got it." Tim ran toward the car and fiddled with some latches holding the second *Specialized* road bike.

Luke sat down on a rock, and wiped away tears. An EMT walked over and looked at his chin. "Let me take a look at that cut, buddy."

Luke nodded approvingly.

While the EMT worked, Evan asked, "How did the crash happen?"

Luke laughed and then pointed to a metal rod on the street, maybe a foot long. "McKnight threw that rod in my spokes. I was in a pack of riders, so when I fell, I took the others with me." He shook his head in disbelief. "I tried to pass him. It was all fun and games until I was in first place."

Evan reached out his hand. "We're not out of this."

"McKnight's gone. Might as well give him the first-place medal right now."

"Good evening, gentlemen," a voice said softly from behind. Evan turned to see their fellow competitor, the American psychologist, Dan Gardner. "I know a way to make up time."

Part II

"O wonder! How many goodly creatures are there here
! How beauteous mankind is! O brave new world that has such people in't."

— William Shakespeare, *The Tempest*

Eighteen

Greenway, Virginia

Evan had been driving for an hour on the sleepy country roads that led toward Mather Gorge, on the border of Maryland and Virginia. The sun was just beginning to set, and the air was moist and cool now. The chill was refreshing as he rolled down his window to let the wind swirl through his car. He welcomed the feeling of peace the rural scenery brought. It was probably the first peace Evan had found since being fired.

Evan rounded a corner and saw a stunning peninsula, which stuck out into the Potomac River almost as an afterthought. Hugging the river were what looked like olive trees. At the edge of the olive grove was a massive house that looked more like a monastery than someone's home. Evan turned into the driveway and drove past a sturdy metal gate attached to a wall of broken stones. The property had a kind of "lost world" feel, as if it were built for another country, another time.

In the distance, Evan saw a figure scurry up the trunk of an olive tree. Evan parked and walked toward what he had seen. As Evan got closer, he could tell it was an older man, maybe in his 70s, though fit enough to climb up and down the gnarled tree trunk easily. Evan passed a garage and saw two pristine road bikes parked inside, and a wetsuit draped over a chair, still dripping wet from a swim.

The walk through the olive grove was enough to make Evan slow down, taking it one step at a time. The summer air hummed with sounds of busy insects—the buzz of grasshoppers, the rolling chants of Cicadas. There was a surreal beauty to the setting, and Evan wondered how long he had gone without this type of respite. Ahead, the man swung a rake-like tool at the tree branches, causing olives to fly in all directions.

The old man was spritely, and in excellent shape for his age. His tanned face was worn though, which seemed to reflect a demanding life. His long, wavy grey hair was pulled back into a ponytail. As Evan approached, the man yanked a flask from the back pocket of his jeans, and took a long swig. His next words were slurred. "You're trespassing on private property, son."

Evan stepped to the edge of a green net that caught falling olives. "Look, we don't know each other, but…"

Ignoring Evan, the man tugged on a branch with bright-green olives. It released and he tossed it toward the net, causing Evan to jump out of the way. The man was clearly drunk.

"You see this tree?" he asked, slapping his hand against the olive tree's trunk. "Olive trees don't grow in Virginia. They're native to the Mediterranean. It's not supposed to be here." He took another drink from his flask, and then lowered his head. "This tree isn't supposed to be here. And neither are you."

Evan said, "I heard you've helped some athletes train for competitions, and I was thinking you could help me—"

"Another wannabe disciple?" He shook his head. "They used to show up at my door in droves. Guys who had read about me, thought I was the answer to their prayers when they'd never done any work in their lives. They wanted to rely on me for something they couldn't do themselves."

Evan bristled at that. He wasn't some athlete who peaked in high school. He had been a star player at a top soccer program in college, and then nearly a professional athlete before quitting. "I'm an athlete—"

The man raised his hand dismissively. "What sport?"

"An ultra-triathlon. Next year in Greece."

"Greece" seemed to register with the man. He shook his head. "Go home, young man."

"I can't."

The man continued to work. "Of course you can. Just stroll back to your car, and—"

Evan dodged the olives sprinkling to the ground. "I was fired."

"From where?"

"A place called the Defense Advanced Research Projects Agency."

The man threw his head back and let out a laugh. "DARPA! Using technology to create the perfect human being. You guys have no idea how to create the perfect anything." He held out a branch. "I have over a thousand olive trees on my land that all have to be harvested. I pick them all by hand. You know why?"

Evan shook his head.

"It's more work, but it produces a superior olive. I pick the olives, sort through the piles, and then throw away any bruised ones." He pointed at a burlap sack filled with olives. It looked heavy. "The best oil comes from hand-picked olives. Shortcuts make for inferior olives." He scoffed. "Scientists like you are all about shortcuts. Your discoveries, your inventions and technology. All just clever shortcuts. And they produce inferior athletes."

Evan wasn't sure he agreed with that. "What makes you so sure?"

"I took those shortcuts. I was kicked out of the Olympics because of it. I was a long-distance runner, a damn good one at that. I remember the first day my coach approached me with his 'enhancements.' I told him to go to hell, but when it became routine, I had to do it to keep up." The man hopped out of the tree, and wobbled as he tried to get his balance. He stuck his finger in the air. "The drugs destroyed my body. Now this washed-up vessel is all that's left. These drugs, technology like yours… all it does is enslave athletes."

"So why didn't you do anything about it?" Evan asked.

"I did!" the man said, raising his arms. "Drugs in sports are out of control. I became an activist; I launched a campaign against performance-enhancing drugs. I wanted to encourage athletes to rebel against their coaches who forced drugs upon them, who were just using them. But nobody listened. They've heard it before, and they still want to win. So I gave up. Left it all behind, bought this land, and have been living a simple, *peaceful* life."

The man chugged more alcohol, and looked at Evan fiercely. "I cheated and lost everything. Take that as a lesson… your *only* lesson." He stumbled back to the tree. "Now get out of here, and never come back."

Nineteen

Dion, Greece

"Make up time?" Evan looked at Dan Gardner incredulously. "You're the Harvard guy, right?"

Gardner chuckled. "Indeed, the Harvard guy. The Galloway brothers, I presume?"

Luke coughed into his hand, and stood up. "You presume correctly."

Gardner handed Luke a water bottle. "Here."

Luke took a sip. "Is this chocolate milk?"

"Ideal for replenishing glycogen stores. Everything the body needs during endurance exercise." Gardner smiled.

Luke obviously had other things to focus on. "You know of a way of catching McKnight?"

Gardner pulled out a detailed map. "I've studied every inch of this course." He pointed to a location on the map and then looked down the dark road. "There is a way through the mountains that will save us fifty miles."

Evan was taken aback. "What kind of way? Like a shortcut?"

Gardner smiled. "McKnight is obviously using a performance enhancer. All I'm saying is that we level the playing field."

Tim showed up with the new bike. "Ready-to-rock."

Luke stood up. "Where does it start?"

"Ten miles up ahead," Gardner said.

"Where's it drop us?"

"Right at the half-way point at Paramythia."

Were they really going to do this? Take a shortcut… *cheat?* Evan started getting that old feeling that he had had in college when his soccer teammates had first started using performance enhancers. He remembered when Lucian told him how he had started. The kneejerk reaction then was "no way," which gave way to a "why not?" which devolved into "screw it." Lucian was a drunk, though. What did he know? And everyone else in the triathlon was gaming the system—McKnight was using Nan Airs, and breaking the rules every chance he got. He thought about what he had done to Julius during the swim. And then there was this crash, how he had treated Luke. Evan's mind flashed back to the night he caught McKnight in bed with Dana. Maybe it was time he stopped being such a boy scout. He was tired of always being the good guy. As McKnight had pointed out, they seem to always finish last. He mounted his bike, and said, "Let's go."

Twenty

Washington, D.C.

The World Economic Forum was not a conference for common men, but a gathering for the elite. Only the rich and powerful attended, including business leaders, former U.S. presidents, princes, and princesses. Each year the world's movers and shakers gathered at this exclusive meeting to discuss the problems of the day. This year it took place in the Eisenhower Executive Building in the US capitol of Washington D.C, where the President's staff worked.

Dana's limo turned onto West Executive Ave., the street between the White House and the Eisenhower Executive Building. She turned to McKnight, who sat beside her smoking a cigar. He was wearing the stupid proud grin he had at the hospital when they were in their twenties, the day Dana delivered McKnight's baby. The same day he had proposed to her, even though she had said no. There were good times, of course, and maybe even love, but Dana had just graduated from medical school and had a promising career ahead of her. The pregnancy was unplanned, and most definitely unwanted. She wasn't ready to be a mother. She didn't *want* to be a mother. And McKnight wasn't the guy for her.

"So the race is in a year," she said, her fixed eyes on the West side of the White House. "When do you plan to begin supplementing with the Nan Airs?"

McKnight pulled his sleeve up, showing puncture wounds at the vein in his forearm.

"Already?" She had no idea he would start so supplementing so early. "How will anyone keep up with you?"

"One or two people might be able to stay close." He chuckled. "Not sure what that boyfriend of yours is trying to prove."

Dana scoffed. "Please, boyfriend? He's a boy."

"He's pretty pissed at me," McKnight said. "He signed up for the Aletheia."

"It's just some 'angry young man' stuff. Don't beat him too bad."

Dana saw a frenzy of media people through the tinted window. She took a piece of paper from one of her pockets, holding it carefully. It was her keynote address.

McKnight looked over at her. "I hear you're getting a lot of calls about Nan Airs?"

McKnight was right. Dana's phone had been ringing off the hook since word had spread about the Nan Airs. "It's become overwhelming."

"It's only going to get worse after your little speech about an 'enhanced Olympics' today."

Dana knew he was right. Given all the badgering she had been subjected to by coaches and athletes, she wished she hadn't agreed to give the keynote address. Dana changed the subject. "I saw the newspaper today. Seems a Chinese scientist had a fatal accident recently?"

McKnight smiled. "Weng was a dangerous loose end. He was too hungry for fame to ever stay quiet. Now only you and I and General Somervell know about the second *Excelsior* project."

Weng would never see his wish for fame come true. Dana tried not to flinch at the casualness with which McKnight talked about killing. She swung a leg out of the car, exposing an athletic thigh through a long slit in her black dress. She walked down the carpet—the left side was swarming with media people; the right was composed of activists, in rebellion against the meeting's theme, which was to consider legalizing performance enhancers in the Olympics. Dana had anticipated such a reaction. Obscenities flew in every direction. Some held signs; others pointed and shouted in disgust. It was a contentious topic, for obvious reasons. With an "enhanced Games," there would be almost no limit to how far the human body could be pushed. It was the only way the Olympic Games would progress, Dana would argue, the only means to ensure that athletes continually broke records.

A crazed woman shoved a sign in her face that said, "Don't play God." Another man held a sign that said, "Cheaters never prosper."

McKnight looked faintly amused. "These guys are really pissed."

There was a sign with an asterisk at the center. Another sign presented a creature with the head of a lion, the body of a goat, and the tail of a serpent. Known as a chimera, it was a critique that enhanced athletes would not be human anymore, but monsters.

A man who looked to be the ringleader glared at Dana as she walked by. "The Greeks first told us about hubris, the consequence of excessive pride, the overconfidence in our abilities. It takes millions of years of evolution to get the enhancements you seek to gain with a simple drug. Only a fool would think they can be controlled."

As Dana and McKnight entered the front entrance of the building, she heard the man continue. "Those who wield these technologies will inevitably fail in their endeavors and they will be destroyed in the process!"

* * *

Dana looked out across the crowd from the podium at the center of the stage. Behind her was an enormous white screen with the title of her keynote address. *Frozen Records: The Future of the Olympics.* She looked over at David Thompson, the President of the International Olympic Committee (IOC). Thompson didn't look pleased. He was outspoken about eradicating performance enhancers from sports.

The screen showed a picture of the Olympic sprinter Usain Bolt, his arms outstretched as he crossed the finish line. It was an image of his record-breaking 100-meter run at the Beijing Olympics. Dana said, "In Beijing, we watched with wonder as Usain Bolt beat his own 100-meter record with a time of 9.69 seconds. A year after, Bolt broke his own record at the World Championships in Athletics in Berlin by more than a tenth of a second.

But how much faster can the 'fastest man on earth' run? How much further can he push his body? Has he—*have we all*—reached the limit of human performance?"

"As DARPA Director, I have had a unique perspective on the evolution of human performance. Or should I say: stagnation. The truth is that the rate of performance improvements is decreasing. Inevitably, they will level off completely, and no records will be broken at all. We won't tolerate inertia. Athletes *must* progress, get better, and continue to mystify us. How will we maintain interest in the Games without the promise of record-breaking performances?"

Dana left a moment for that to sink in. "Records will stagnate unless we modify our athletes. Technology has already found its way into nearly every sport. Swimmers improve their glide in the water with suits made of advanced fabrics. Runners reduce their drag with fabric designed with dimples around the arms and legs. We are in the age of biological technology, ladies and gentlemen. With cutting-edge advancements in labs such as DARPA's, we can engineer whole new categories of athletes. We can unlock new levels of human potential to usher in an exciting time of unparalleled human competitiveness, a new era in sports."

A delegate stood up. "What about the long-term health effects of biological enhancements? Think about the doping program in East Germany. Those athletes are falling apart today."

Dana raised her hands, expecting such objections. "Prudence is necessary, of course. All modifications would be tested for safety and medically supervised."

"The Games are dirty enough!" another man shouted from the back.

Dana pointed to the man. "Doping is already so prevalent, so why shouldn't we legalize it, make performance enhancers available to everyone?"

"I suppose we just pass out anabolic steroids and erythropoietin like candy?" one of the delegates asked.

"These supplements are small-time. We have technologies at DARPA that will dazzle spectators for years to come."

David Thompson stood up. He was an imposing man, a former Olympian. "What about the integrity of sports, Dr. Brines? Whatever happened to good old-fashioned training?"

"Purists?" Dana said. "They won't be able to keep up. More to the point, they already can't keep up. I'm not just saying that they will be dinosaurs, but that they already are. We need to recognize that."

Thompson didn't look convinced. "And what if the athletes refuse to take your drugs?"

Dana glanced at McKnight in the crowd. "There was a study in the 1980s that asked athletes to consider a hypothetical drug that would guarantee them a gold medal in the Olympics. The majority said they would use it, despite potential negative health effects." Dana paused dramatically. Now she was speaking directly to McKnight. "Athletes won't refuse the opportunity to be bigger, faster, and stronger. The obsession with winning is too profound. Glory is too important."

* * *

After Dana's talk, the event's attendees gathered in the main lobby of the Eisenhower Building. The room was formally decorated, looking like it might have come from a hundred years ago or more. On the tables were eighteenth-century silverware, nestled beside exquisite china and glistening crystal. Waiters carried trays with smoked-fish salad and tart za'atar, filling half-empty wine glasses to the brim. Off to the side was a cello quartet playing selections from Vivaldi's Four Seasons.

With a vodka tonic in hand, Dana stood at the center a group composed of several well-dressed members of the International Olympics Committee, including David Thompson. While they sipped cocktails, Dana delivered her elevator speech about DARPA's advanced technologies with deft persuasion. Occasionally, she would glance at the spot across the room where McKnight was speaking with the head of the advisory panel for the World Anti-Doping Agency, a man named Masterson.

Around Dana, the delegates discussed the benefits of her proposals. An intellectual-looking man with a flat voice seemed enthusiastic.

"The games have become rather anemic. Perhaps a little enhanced games-manship *would* do them some good."

"I agree," another said. "The Olympic Games are a theater. Modification would certainly enhance the drama for spectators and make for a better spectacle."

Of the IOC members there, only Thompson didn't seem to be buying Dana's pitch. "Maybe we should slap engines on cyclists' road bikes, too?"

"I understand your hesitation," Dana said, "But what happens when world records become untouchable, and the games become as exciting as watching grass grow?"

"Training regimens will evolve, nutrition programs will improve, coaches will-"

"Coaches are sheep," Dana said, cutting him off. "Training and nutrition have reached the point where they are no longer producing results. We *must* embrace new technology."

"I think you underestimate elite athletes," Thompson said. "They're not pawns on a chessboard. No Olympian I know will agree to using your technology."

"*You* are underestimating them, David," Dana shot back. "You underestimate Olympians' drive to succeed. They will do whatever it takes to win."

Thompson leaned in close to Dana. The difficulty was that Thompson was a man of honor. "The simple fact is, *Dr. Brines*, I would rather see the stands empty than have the Olympic fields swarming with cheats."

Dana was bored. She nodded to McKnight, and lifted her empty glass. "Gentlemen, I need a refill." Everyone but Thompson smiled widely. As Dana walked away, Thompson narrowed his eyes with skepticism.

There was a tap on Dana's shoulder. She spun around to see a wild-looking man with beady eyes, wearing jeans and a black sweatshirt, the hood pulled over his head. Dana tiptoed backward, but the man came in close enough that she could feel the hot air from his mouth.

"I need Nan Airs," he said with an unblinking gaze.

Dana glanced over the man's shoulder and saw two guards making their way through the crowd toward them. "Look, buddy, I'm not thinking your name's on the invitation list, so I suggest—"

He grabbed her by the collar. "Just one vial!"

Dana was frightened, but the guards snatched the man back. She watched him being dragged away. She couldn't help but think how pathetic his fervor for Nan Airs was. She was so tired of the countless requests for Nan Airs over the phone, or email, or sometimes a desperate visit at DARPA's doorstep. This was the first time Dana had seen the allure of Nan Airs up close. The potential the drug delivered was potent. It created monsters.

McKnight stood beside Masterson. He introduced the gangly-looking man. "Dana, this is Dr. Masterson, the head of the advisory panel for the World Anti-Doping Agency." Masterson shoveled a piece of sushi into his mouth, and stuck out his hand.

"Pleased to meet you." Dana took his hand. While he was a slob, he had a remarkable resume.

McKnight gestured to the other man. "Masterson is a former geneticist at Yale. Now he works with the government, ensuring that performance enhancers stay out of sports."

Unless of course the opposite made him rich. Dana didn't need to ask to know that the man was corrupt, a puppet in McKnight's games to evade being caught using in an event with sophisticated drug testing. Such a corrupt man could be an asset. But how could she use him?

Twenty-One

Athens, Greece

It was two days before the opening ceremony of the Olympic Games. Dana's helicopter hovered over the Spiros Louis Stadium, which was already buzzing with pre-ceremony activity. Through her headphones she heard an NBC commentator start to talk.

"Over 3,000 athletes from almost 100 countries have come to Athens for the start of this year's Summer Games. Twenty-eight sports will be represented; three hundred medals are up for grabs. And, of course, there's the *Aletheia*, which will culminate just six miles west of the city at the summit of Egaleo Mountain. The winner of the epic 700-mile triathlon will then ride by chariot into the stadium for the honor of carrying the Olympic torch the final steps to light the flame."

Dana thought back to the covert conversation she had initiated with Masterson at the Davos meeting after McKnight had wandered away. Seeing the athlete there who had accosted her had just been confirmation of what she needed to do. She'd known that the IOC would never agree to her proposal, but it was necessary to at least appear to be in favor of doping for things to progress the way she wanted.

The conversation with Masterson had been shockingly candid, and productive. For $250,000, Masterson agreed to expose McKnight to the world by testing his blood for Nan Airs during the race. But Masterson had help with so much more.

The only roadblock was Thompson, of course. "I hear that that Thompson's launched a multi-million dollar campaign to upgrade their testing methods to detect performance-enhancing drugs," Dana had said. The real question hung unspoken.

Will next-generation tests detect Nan Airs?

Masterson was chomping on a piece of sushi then, and checked to see that McKnight was out of earshot. "Their technology is years behind the curve." Masterson wiped his mouth and grinned. "It appears you and I live in the same world, Dr. Brines."

"And what world is that?"

"A world of gray."

Masterson had made quick work of the plan. Dana provided the Nan Airs; Masterson distributed them. Nearly every country eventually requested Nan Airs, America included. They had fallen like dominoes.

As to whether her plans were "right" or "wrong," Dana had begun to think that sometimes you must do a little bad to do a lot of good. Making cheaters pay seemed to be the *absolute* good. Ridding sports of unethical athletes was morally important enough to justify the means of achieving it. McKnight personified the immoral athlete, but to treat him as the only one was ludicrous. She thought about how he would enter the stadium a conquering hero, and then, minutes later be doubled-over, coughing blood… dying. Most importantly, it would happen in front of a global audience. According to NBC, approximately twenty million people would watch the opening ceremony. McKnight would finally have his global stage.

Dana checked the time. McKnight was likely in Paramythia by now, the half-way point in the triathlon's cycling portion. She turned the radio down, grabbed her satellite phone, and called McKnight's cell phone.

* * *

Paramythia, Greece

Staring into a roaring fire, Evan picked at a steaming plate of pasta and potatoes on his lap. It was early morning, and the sun would rise soon. Though ravenous, he couldn't eat. The decision to take the shortcut had caught him up to the race's leaders, McKnight included, but it was gnawing at him, leaving him with a sinking feeling in his stomach. He had made up the time, but he was having trouble living with it.

"How's your brother?" Isabella sat on the seat next to Evan. "He was in that accident, right?"

Evan was silent. He was far away, lost in thought.

She waved a hand in front of his face. "Earth to Evan."

Evan blinked rapidly. "Sorry."

He gave Isabella a blank look. She was gorgeous in the dim light, enchanting, in fact. Her dark brown hair was in a bun, her outfit exposed athletic shoulders and arms, and her eyes were bright and inquisitive.

"Your brother—"

"Yes, yeah, he's okay." Evan produced a fake smile. "Thank you for asking." Evan managed a bite of bread. When Evan had seen Isabella on the beach, he was confident, self-assured. The decision to take the shortcut had left him feeling ashamed, disempowered. Isabella must be able to sense it. Should he admit it? That he had cheated?

She scooted down the seat toward Evan. "Something wrong?"

Evan washed a hand down his face. "I just need some sleep."

Isabella smelled of sweat, but her perfume lingered. The mixture was intoxicating. "I saw you help Julius in the water. You're a good person for doing that, you know. Everyone else just swam by him."

A good person, Evan thought. He wasn't so sure.

Isabella ran her fingers through her hair. Her lips were wet, inviting. The timing was perfect to make a move, Evan thought. Early morning. They were the only athletes awake. A warm fire, dim light. Two attractive, fit, and adventurous people…

"Mr. Galloway," a man said, interrupting Evan's train of thought.

Evan turned to see Masterson.

Masterson's expression was cold. "It's time for your mandatory drug test."

Twenty-Two

It had been at least a year since Evan had handled a soccer ball, like the one in the passenger side seat of his car. It had felt good to juggle it before he left for Lucian's house. He thought if only Lucian could see Evan's skills, he might understand he was an athlete. Maybe then he would accept him as a student. This meeting would go better. *It had to.*

Lucian was intimidatingly fit, especially for his age, way better shape than Evan. Evan's muscles were clunky from neglect, and didn't respond like they had in college. He was carrying twenty extra pounds of fat, mostly around his belly. His cardiovascular fitness was a joke. Before he had left for Lucian's, he had tried a few sprints, but found himself winded after a couple minutes. There was a time when his VO2max was in the high 60s, the mark of an elite athlete. It was likely to be in the low 40s now, perhaps even 30s, a shameful number given his athletic experience.

Evan was daunted by the fact that, in one year's time, he would have to run the equivalent of almost six marathons—*after* swimming 12 miles and biking 560. He thought about asking Luke if he wanted to train together, but he knew his brother was too competitive for that. Luke already thought Evan was trying to steal his thunder by participating in the Aletheia. And then there was the pain of their father's death, present anytime they were together. About five minutes from Lucian's house, Evan scrolled through the contacts in his cell phone, found his brother's number, and pressed send.

"What's up?" There was rustling on Luke's side of the phone. He was in a hurry.

Evan mustered a "nothing," and there was an awkward pause. "How's training?"

More rustling. "First day, actually. Having a peanut butter and jelly sandwich before I head out for a workout."

"I was wondering if you wanted to train together sometime."

Luke snorted. "C'mon man, you couldn't keep up with me."

Evan knew he was right. He was out of shape, and Luke was the picture of fitness. The days of big brother dominating every sibling rivalry had long passed.

"You really have no idea what you got yourself into, do you? I've been competing in ultras for three years now, and it'll take everything I've got to just *finish* this one." There was a pause. "Look man, I can't talk about that right now."

He thought it best to not push Luke on the matter. There was a time and place for such conversations. "What's your training looking like today?"

Luke was matter-of-fact. "Brick workout: fifty-mile bike ride, six-mile run."

Evan turned his car into Lucian's driveway. Those distances seemed incomprehensible.

"Heard you have some extra time on your hands these days," Luke said.

"How'd you know I was fired?"

Luke stuttered. "You told me, right?"

"No, I didn't."

"Well at least you can use that time to train."

Evan didn't know how Luke found out, but he decided to drop that, too. "I'm trying to get this ex-triathlete to train me. Some guru."

"Who?" Luke seemed suddenly interested in the conversation; jealous perhaps?

"My old soccer coach recommended this guy from Greece. Name's Lucian."

"Lucian Atticus?"

"Yeah, how did you—"

"Guy's a legend in the ultra-circuit. I should say *was* a legend. There was an article in *Outside Magazine* about him a few years ago, called him the 'Tiger Woods' of Greece until the anti-doping agency caught him and he got banned. So he came to the States and made a name for himself in triathlons."

Evan parked his car in front of Lucian's garage. He scanned the olive grove for the old man, but there was no sign. "You said he did ultra-triathlons?"

"I've done some pretty gnarly races, but this guy takes it to a whole other level. He's won the Ironman World Championship three times. He won the Tour d' Afrique—a 6,800-mile bike ride across Africa. He ran the Badwater Ultramarathon every year, which is 135 miles nonstop from Death Valley to Mount Whitney in temperatures up to 130 degrees. The ground gets so hot the glue in your shoes melts."

Evan knew the demands such endurance exercises put on the body. It took major thermoregulatory adaptations and a bulletproof mental attitude to run in 130 degrees for 135 miles on ground over 100 degrees hot. "Guy's the real deal, huh?"

Luke didn't sound impressed anymore. "He wanted to get back in the Olympics. He started this pathetic anti-doping campaign, but that was put down pretty quickly. So Helmsley recommended him to you?"

"Yeah."

"Figures he would."

Evan knew Luke never approved of Helmsley's blatant abuse of substances, even though he had ultimately fallen victim himself. "I'm going to see if he will train me."

"Good luck with that," Luke said. "Apparently people are always showing up at his doorstep, asking to train with him, like he's the messiah or something. He gave it up after some of his disciples doped themselves. These days, he's just a drunk."

Evan saw a figure through the olive trees. It was Lucian. "I see him, gotta go."

Luke sounded shocked. "You're at his house?"

"Later, man." Evan hung up, and stepped out of his car. Lucian was still wet from a swim, carrying swimming goggles, wearing a skin-tight wetsuit peeled down to his hips. His body showed obvious signs of aging, but his chest was broad, muscular.

He spotted Evan. "I thought I told you never to come back here."

Evan walked alongside Lucian as he headed for his garage. The walls of the garage were covered in athletic equipment, including two pristine road bikes, helmets, and wetsuits. A Timex watch sat on the workbench with more goggles, and Bodyglide to lubricate chafe-prone parts of the body during racing.

"Look," Evan said, "I know you think I am a joke, but—"

"No, you're not a joke; you're a fool." Lucian tossed his goggles onto the bench. "A joke would be a *marathoner* asking for training, maybe someone who had done a triathlon *before* signing up for a quintuple ultra-triathlon." He pointed to Evan's gut. "Look at this spare tire around your waist. You gonna fill your water bottles with diet soda?"

Evan knew he had a long way to go, but he wasn't going to back down. He stood solidly, determined. "I can do this. I know I can."

That was enough to make Lucian pause. "Make me believe. Prove to me that you've got some athleticism, and that you can summon it at will. Then I'll *think* about training you."

"I'll be right back." Evan jogged to his car. He quickly put on soccer boots and then grabbed his ball. He ran back to Lucian, ball under his arm. His muscles felt tight, but his mind was sharp.

The old man laughed. "I've never seen a soccer ball in a triathlon."

Evan ignored him. He stepped on the ball with his right foot, rolled it into his left foot, and popped it up a foot off the ground. He tapped the ball higher with his left foot then circled the same up and under it. Just before the ball hit the ground, he tapped it from his left foot to his right. Then he began juggling, passing the ball back and forth between his feet about waist high.

Evan glanced at Lucian for approval, but the older man stood unimpressed. Evan moved forward, still juggling the ball between his feet. Evan was out of shape, but he still knew a fair share of tricks. The "Robino pullback" looked pretty nifty, and often got players out of tight spaces. Evan tapped the ball from his left foot to his right. He lifted his right foot toward his left, and then swept it back and caught the ball with this right. He did that five times in a row. Lucian was not having it, however. Evan had to go bigger, and prepared himself for a "seal dribble." He tapped the ball onto his left foot and kicked it up high up over his head. He bounced the ball off his forehead and ran forward. He crossed the driveway bouncing the ball repeatedly off his forehead.

"Amusing," Lucian said in an indifferent tone. "Anything else in that bag of tricks?"

Evan was frustrated. Perhaps the "rainbow" would get his attention. He backed up to the edge of the driveway and started running, the ball skipping across the ground. At full speed, he squeezed the ball between both his feet behind him. The ball launched it into the air, sailed over his head, and landed in front of him. Evan stopped in front of Lucian, looking hopeful.

Lucian pointed to a thick olive tree about fifteen feet high. "I want you to kick the ball from here to the center of that tree, and bounce it back like a boomerang. If you can do that, I will train you. If you can't, well, you know your way out."

The tree was easily thirty feet away. It was *not* possible. "From here? No way."

"And do it three times in a row."

Evan was floored. Only a handful of professional soccer players had the skill to kick the ball from the goal line to the goalpost and bounce it back. But Evan knew he couldn't get ready for this triathlon without a trainer like Lucian. He faced the tree squarely, and took a deep breath.

"One more thing," Lucian said. "The ball can't hit the ground."

Evan dropped his shoulders. *"What?"*

Lucian folded his arms across his chest.

Evan didn't dare say anything else in case the old man just made the challenge harder. He inhaled deeply and focused his gaze on the tree. The tree split into two large branches about ten feet up. To get it to ricochet back, he would have to hit the split with precision. He began juggling, trying to suppress an avalanche of self-doubt. He glanced at the tree once more, tapped the ball as high as his chest, and then struck it at its lowest point. The ball shot away with astonishing speed. Evan watched it strike the split perfectly and rebound in his direction. But it was coming in low, and he had to lunge desperately to barely get the tip of his foot underneath it. The ball flipped into the air. Evan bounced it off his knee, and continued juggling. Evan felt a rush of adrenaline; he felt awake for the first time in a very long time.

He looked at Lucian. The old man was grinning. Within seconds, the ball was sailing at the tree again. It ricocheted back and Evan trapped it with his chest and let it drop to his foot. *One more time*, he thought. The world fell away, and he booted the ball with everything he had. The ball hit the split tree and bounced back in a slow, perfect arc.

Lucian stepped into the ball's path and caught it with both hands.

"What are you doing?" Evan asked with surprise.

"It will take a full year of training to get ready for this race. It will take total devotion. And if you do not give it everything, you will fail. Be here tomorrow, 6 AM." He tossed the soccer ball at Evan.

Evan caught it, out of breath and not knowing what to say.

"You will stay at my house. So pack for a year."

Twenty-Three

Athens, Greece

"Hello, dear," Dana said. There was nothing endearing about her tone.

McKnight's voice was groggy. "Dana… hi… I was sleeping." There was a pause. "What is it? What is that noise?"

"I'm in a helicopter over the stadium in Athens."

"I've gotta get on the bike in a few hours, Dana. What do you want?"

"Have you heard of the Erinyes, Jack?"

McKnight sounded annoyed. "Rings a bell, I guess."

"The Erinyes were goddesses," she said, matter-of-factly. "In Greek, *Erinys* means 'the avengers.'"

"What the hell does this have to do with anything?"

"The Erinyes were avengers of crime and wickedness. They were also called *the Furies*. They would wait beneath the ground, and then rise up and punish those who had sworn a false oath."

McKnight sounded more awake now. "What are you talking about? What are you up to, Dana?"

"You have a debt to pay, Jack." She was cold, unforgiving. "Look out your window."

"*What?*"

"What do you see?"

There was rustling through the phone. "Masterson's doing his rounds. He's talking to Evan now. Not that he'll find anything with him." Her tone was sarcastic. "That one's pure as the driven snow."

She knew McKnight was watching Masterson draw Evan's blood and then run it through an anti-doping test. "You see that blood test that Masterson's using? That test *can* detect respirocytes. Masterson has betrayed you, Jack. Soon, he will knock on your door. He will discover Nan Airs in your bloodstream, and then he will disqualify you from the race."

McKnight stuttered. "How… wait—?"

Dana smiled. The shame for McKnight would be tremendous. He had it coming for all the times he'd cheated. His most horrific crime was, of course, sacrificing Michael in the Great Wall Marathon. Merely exposing him wouldn't be enough for that.

"Our own son," she said. "What you did was unspeakable."

McKnight whimpered. "Weng said he could reverse it. I didn't know he was going to die."

Dana relished hearing him squirm like a caged animal. McKnight would do or say anything to get himself off the hook. Not this time, though.

"Please Dana, tell him to stop. If this gets out, I'll be ruined."

Dana laughed. "Oh, Jack, you're always quoting ancient wisdom; here's one: 'Let thy punishment fit the crime.'"

McKnight couldn't form complete sentences. "I…" he coughed. "I trusted you. I thought we were together again. I thought you loved me."

Dana didn't have to harden her heart. Her son's death had done that. "You're a fool, Jack. I played the part, gave you the woman you needed, made you fall in love all over again. All so I could punish you for what you did."

Dana heard a knock through the phone. Masterson had arrived.

"Dana?" McKnight said with desperation.

"Goodbye, Jack."

Twenty-Four

At first, the idea of living with Lucian seemed absurd. Why couldn't he just drive to his house every morning? But, in the end, Evan understood that preparing for the challenge would require total commitment. Only total immersion would allow him to focus single-mindedly on training. It was 5:48 AM when Evan returned to Lucian's house, his car full of a year's worth of possessions. A sliver of knee-high mist hovered over the olive grove, and while the sun was still settled below the horizon, there was a brilliant orange glow behind the clouds over the Potomac.

Lucian was harvesting olives, as always it seemed. Evan approached, and Lucian hopped down. He looked over Evan's shoulder at the Volvo stuffed with bags and boxes.

Evan said, "I guess I'm yours now."

"A poor man once approached Socrates looking to be mentored. The man said, 'I am a poor man and have nothing else to give, but offer you myself.'"

"What'd Socrates say?"

"Do you not see that you are offering me the greatest gift of all?"

Evan suspected these quips would come frequently.

"So, what's it going to be today," Evan said, "run, bike, or swim?"

Lucian handed Evan tree clippers. "Today, we harvest olives."

Evan rolled the rusty tool around in his hands. "Come again?"

Lucian pointed to a heap of rolled-up nets. "First, cover the orchard with those nylon nets. Then you can knock the olives from the trees."

Evan frowned. "I came here to train for an ultra-triathlon, not do yard work."

Lucian's face became stern. "If you want even a shred of a chance in Greece, you will do everything I say from here on out. Are we clear?"

Evan slumped. "Okay, okay."

Lucian pulled a flask from his jacket and took a swig. His face contorted as the alcohol went down.

Evan stared at him. "It's a little early for that, don't you think?"

Lucian pointed at the nets, and took another pull.

* * *

It had taken Evan two hours of back-breaking work to cover the olive orchard's hundreds of square feet with nets. After unrolling the nets, he cut holes for the trunks, letting them poke through. The grove was on a hillside, so Evan worked on a slant, climbing up and down as he worked. After the netting was in place, he set rocks at each corner to keep them in position, but he tripped over the nets constantly, pulling up the material with his feet. Each time he did, he would have to backtrack, and reposition the net. Tree branches and thorns often punctured the net as well, which meant he had to patch up the holes with Duct Tape.

Around mid-day, Evan finally climbed into the trees, but the work wasn't any easier. The heat had climbed into the 80s and his clothes were drenched with sweat. His hands were covered in dirt, and his fingernails became dark and cracked.

From below, Lucian watched impassively. "The olives are on the small branches."

To release the olives, Evan whipped the branches with a thick dowel. It was satisfying to watch them fly off the branches and rain into the nets.

"Prune with more force," Lucian said, like a father disciplining his son. "Like you're mad at it!"

Lucian meandered away, grabbing a sip of booze here and there. Evan wondered how many hours Lucian had spent in these trees, and what sorrows he had tried to wash away through the labor. As the day wore on, the old man became more intoxicated. No doubt he had been devastated after he lost his status in Greece as a professional athlete. Lucian had a beautiful home in an idyllic setting, but it appeared meaningless to him, just an elaborate existence at rock bottom.

Evan didn't feel particularly safe high in the trees. Occasionally, a weak branch would snap under his body weight, and he would grab wildly for anything to stop his fall.

Lucian laughed at his request for a safety harness. "You will experience far more danger in that race," he said. "You need to become comfortable with being on the edge."

With practice, Evan learned to control the rush of adrenaline a near fall gave him, even relish it at times. Despite a few close calls, it was peaceful in the trees. When he was really high—around twenty-five feet—the tree swayed in the hot breeze, and he found himself rocking with it gently, losing himself momentarily. When the sun reached its highest point in the sky, it reflected a kaleidoscope of greens, yellows, and oranges off Black Pond. Evan watched a falcon float on a thermal above the pond. Occasionally, fish would leap at the edges.

After knocking the olives to the nets, Lucian commanded Evan to climb down from the trees. He told him to roll the olives to the middle of the nets, and then pick through them on his hands and knees.

"Hand-sorting yields the best quality olives," the man said.

Evan still wasn't certain what harvesting olives had to do with a triathlon, but he obeyed his new teacher. As Evan gathered olives on his knees, Lucian hovered over him. "There are no shortcuts... not in a harvest, not in triathlons, not in life. It's all just hard work."

When Evan spotted a healthy olive, he placed it in a satchel around his waist. When a satchel was full, he brought it to a crate, which was only half-filled by early afternoon. Lucian didn't look impressed as he inspected the crate.

Evan began to tire by 4 PM. Exhausted and frustrated, he finally asked the question that had been building in him all day. "What the hell does picking olives have to do with a triathlon?"

Lucian chuckled and took a swig from his flask. "Are you thirsty?

Evan nodded.

"Blood sugar feel low? Muscles weak? Feel like you're overheating?"

Evan nodded again.

Lucian leaned against a tree. "Olive trees aren't that different from athletes. They produce higher-quality fruit when they are stressed. The harder I push you, the stronger you will be. Like the olives, I want a superior product."

∗ ∗ ∗

Lucian's house, built in a style of a Mediterranean villa, was enormous. Evan carried a burlap sack over his shoulder as Lucian led him down the driveway. He admired the small bushes trimmed into human figures, including an athlete throwing a javelin, another holding a shot-put against its chin. They passed marble columns at the front door and entered a foyer on the middle floor. The house was three stories high with two floors of rooms, a loft above the living room. Lucian led Evan across the living room, which had pine-paneled walls and brown oak floors. There was a bust of Plato on the mantle.

"You're really living the good life," Evan said, admiring the collected artwork and sculptures that lined the walls, and the grand circular fireplace at the center of the room. Covering the windows were long silk curtains, sashayed with golden ropes. Evan also noticed a small library and a sunlit solarium off the living room, which led to a courtyard and a landscaped garden.

Lucian pointed to a long dining room table covered with food. "Sit."

Evan felt his stomach grumble. "What's on the menu?"

Lucian's speech was slurred by now. "Amberjack Carpaccio with king crab and black eyed peas with fennel salsa." Evan sat and Lucian went on, "We'll be eating a Mediterranean diet for your training. This includes fresh and natural ingredients from local fruit and vegetable farms. It's a lifestyle, a healthy way of living."

Evan could barely listen, he was so hungry. He launched into the meal, shoveling food into his mouth with abandon.

"Whoa, whoa, whoa," Lucian said, raising a hand. "Slow down. Pay attention as you eat. Let the tastes linger."

Evan slowed his chewing, and indeed the flavors on his tongue became more pronounced. Lucian broke apart a piece of crusty bread, and dabbed it into a bowl of olive oil. Looking at the bottle of oil, he said, "People look at that bottle and have no idea what went into it. You have some idea now."

Evan nodded. "It's no picnic, that's for sure."

"Neither will be getting your body into the shape it needs to be in for this triathlon." Lucian seemed almost to come into focus as he said it. "Like I said in the grove, you will need to become very tolerant of pain. In an ultra-event, you'll become dehydrated, you'll cramp and chaff, your feet will blister, and toe nails will fall off. You will constantly worry about whether you are consuming enough calories and water, whether you are going to get lost, or your pace is fast enough. Your body will want to give up, so you must always guard your mental faculties fiercely. Once they go, you go."

Lucian set his flask on the kitchen counter and grabbed a bottle of wine. He poured the wine into a glass carelessly, the wine missing the glass at times, splashing across the marble counter. After he managed to fill the glass to the brim, he washed down two gulps before sitting down beside Evan. The aroma of alcohol was strong.

Evan knew the Mediterranean diet called for red wine—the antioxidants in the wine were natural anti-inflammatories and had proven health benefits—but that was in moderation. Lucian was Evan's coach, but Evan thought perhaps he would have to prop his trainer up as well.

Lucian took a bite of crab. "To win a race like this, you don't just need exceptional endurance, or great mental toughness. You must become a superior man."

Evan stopped mid-chew, skeptical. "A superior man?"

"I know about your soccer game. You caught the cross, when you could have easily kicked it in."

Apparently, Lucian had done his homework.

"It's the only reason I offered to train you. You have potential in ways none of my other students had."

Evan continued eating. "That game cost me everything."

"But you didn't compromise yourself. You did the right thing. This is what I mean by a superior man. I don't just mean physical perfection. Confucius said, 'The way of the superior man is threefold. Virtuous, he is free from anxieties. Wise, he is free from perplexities. And bold, he is free from fear.'"

"Were you a 'superior man'?"

Lucian looked uncomfortable. "A long time ago. Before I turned into something else."

Evan hung his head. "I once broke the rules, too. I used performance enhancers in college."

Lucian obviously hadn't expected that, but he seemed to understand it. "You probably thought 'why not,' since everyone else was doing it?"

"Yes."

"And then you felt shame?"

"I did."

"You wanted to do the right thing, so you caught that ball…"

"I told my coach I was done the day before. I couldn't take feeling bad about it anymore. And my brother was following my lead. If I approved, he approved."

"You made a mistake. Humans aren't perfect." Lucian took a big gulp of wine. "We are fundamentally *imperfect*. You felt shame, because who you were was inconsistent with who you wanted to be. But, my friend, that's where moral progress starts—with shame in your inconsistency."

"Why did you stop training athletes?"

Lucian spread his hands along the table. "We live in an age of inferior men, Evan. An age where politicians only care about their careers, where accountants make up balance sheets, where banks exploit honest, hard-working people, and where rocket scientists become stock brokers just to get rich quick. Self-centeredness, greed, deceit. Scandal after scandal. Inferior men."

Evan thought these 'inferior men' sounded an awful lot like McKnight.

"And what about athletes?"

Lucian looked sullen. "Some of the worst offenders."

"If it's so pervasive, why fight it?"

Lucian glanced at the bust of Plato on the mantle. "Plato said that the ideal starting point for creating a city of law is a tyranny."

Evan finished his dinner, and Lucian led him across the living room and up a curved staircase to a loft that had a clear view to the Potomac. "You'll sleep here," Lucian said, pointing to a twin-size bed that looked as if it had never been touched. "Training starts tomorrow."

Lucian was at the top of the stairs when Evan asked, "These athletes you trained... who were they?"

There was contempt in Lucian's voice. "The last athlete I trained was Jack McKnight. Now get some rest. You're going to need it."

Twenty-Five

Paramythia, Greece

McKnight's fingers were shaking so badly that he had difficulty keeping the cigarette to his lips. He hadn't smoked in a decade, not since he first got into endurance sports. He took a nervous puff and blew out smoke, scanning the inside of his trailer, which was in disarray from the fight.

Lying on the kitchen floor was a corpse, its head shattered and leaking dark-red blood. It had all happened so fast. Masterson had entered the trailer and was swift in his judgment, saying that McKnight was using Nan Airs and that his time was up. "Once I call the race officials," Masterson had said, "you'll be disqualified."

"Wait a minute," McKnight had said urgently, raising his hands. "Whatever Dana's paying you, I'll double it."

"Tempting." Masterson circled the interior cautiously. "But, no deal. It just wouldn't be right letting you win this way."

"So you're going to rat me out, is that it? Get me kicked out of the race? When did you start caring about whether someone was using?"

"When I started my career," Masterson snapped back. "Men like you took that from me inch by inch. Those fans out there with your face on their signs will finally see who you really are. Not a hero, but a cautionary tale."

"And Dana?"

"Dana's got bigger plans. I met with Olympic coaches. They took to Nan Airs like flies to shit. And the athletes are passing the drug around like it's Gatorade."

McKnight shook his head. "Okay, I don't care about any of that. I just want to finish this race, alright? Let me do that, *please*."

Masterson pulled a cell phone from his pocket to make the call. "Jack, do you think I'm going to let you just get back on your bike and finish?"

McKnight lowered to his knees and clasped his hands together. "Don't do this."

"For the first time in your life, Jack," Masterson said, bringing the phone to his ear, "You're going to fail."

The next two minutes were a blur in McKnight's mind. Even as he took the last drag off his cigarette and watched the sun rise through a window, he had to keep looking at Masterson's lifeless body to confirm that it had all really happened.

McKnight had lunged at Masterson, his hands outstretched. Masterson toppled backward, and his cell phone skipped across the floor. McKnight mounted him and wrapped his hands around the man's neck. Masterson's arms flapped wildly as his airway closed off. His hands searched the floor, finding one of McKnight's bike shoes. He swung it into McKnight's face. The metal spikes sunk into his flesh, and McKnight cried out in agony. With more force, Masterson struck again and McKnight toppled off, covering his face in horror.

The spikes had drawn blood, and one had struck McKnight's eye. He felt blood seep from puncture holes and his right eye felt popped. Masterson scurried across the floor on his hands and knees. McKnight hopped onto his back and punched him in the back of the head repeatedly. Masterson looked stunned, but when McKnight let up, he lashed out with a butter knife on the floor. McKnight wailed as it sank into his leg. Tears filled his eyes and he trembled with rage. He grabbed Masterson by the neck, snatched his bike helmet, and his mind went blank. He lifted the helmet high and bludgeoned Masterson's head. Again and again and again.

McKnight had done despicable things in his life, but never murder. Never directly. Even with his son, Dr. Weng had been the one to do everything—the blood wasn't on his hands.

McKnight's wounded leg shook uncontrollably. Without thinking, he quickly yanked the knife from his leg. He tore off his shirt and tied it tight around his thigh, slowing the bleeding. How would he race now? His right eye had fully closed shut, leaving him with one working eye. He grabbed Masterson's ankle and dragged the body into the center of the trailer. He wrapped his body in a bed sheet and looked out the window to see if anyone was still awake. Everyone had gone to sleep, including Evan. He lifted the body onto his shoulder and tiptoed out the back door. A few hundred feet from his trailer was a ledge that dropped off into a deep gorge. It would be the perfect place to dump the body. When McKnight reached the edge, he lifted the body off his shoulder and heaved it into the blackness. The corpse struck the side of the cliff, but he didn't hear it hit the bottom.

When McKnight entered the trailer, he hurried to a mirror. What he saw horrified him. The right side of his face had been mutilated, and his right eye was destroyed. He almost didn't even care about his leg. He would have sacrificed *any* other part of his body but his face. It was his greatest asset—his winning smile, chiseled jawline, sparkling eyes, all of which were crucial to winning negotiations, persuading clients, and wooing women. The man in the mirror was disfigured, a freak. Could he finish the race with one working eye? He had to try.

He rummaged through a drawer underneath the sink and found a first aid kit. He found a bottle of aspirin and popped four pills. Then he used gauze pads to absorb the blood dripping from the puncture holes on his face. When the wounds were clean, he applied hydrogen peroxide and winced from the sting. He attached Band-Aids and then continued searching through the kit, pushing aside bandages, scissors, dressings, and adhesive tape. Finally, he saw what he needed. He lifted the eye patch up to the mirror. He pressed it to his eye socket and tied the string in the back.

As he washed Masterson's dried blood off his hands, he felt that something inside him had shifted. Darkness gripped him. All that mattered now was winning the *Aletheia*. And he would do anything to make sure it happened.

Twenty-Six

Evan woke to loud noises from the kitchen below. Was it really the first day? Was he really going to train for a 700-mile triathlon? He was an initiate now, and would have to put himself faithfully in the hands of his "guru." A part of him wanted to leap out of bed and skip downstairs. Starting anything—whether a diet, a workout program, a new relationship—was exciting, but he was hesitant in the warmth of his bed. The whole task seemed too large, unmanageable. Impossible. He had spent most of his twenties studying the human body's potential in the confines of the Ivory Tower, and he knew the limits better than anyone. Evan knew more theory than Lucian, but the old man had lived that theory. Evan's mind swirled with thoughts of Dana and McKnight together, his brother's recklessness...

"Get up!" Lucian's voice was booming.

Evan scurried out of bed, and saw a 2XU "tri" singlet folded neatly on the floor. It was made to be worn throughout an entire triathlon. It was lightweight, quick-drying, and tight-fitting for aerodynamics. He squeezed into it, grabbed his duffel bag, and jogged downstairs. Lucian had set food out, including a bowl of oatmeal with banana slices and chocolate chips.

"Morning," Evan said, rubbing his eyes. The clock on the wall read *5:05 AM*.

Lucian placed a cup on the table filled with a dark-red liquid. "Hope you like beet juice."

Many elite endurance athletes drank beet juice to increase oxygen uptake and efficiency, and therefore stamina. It was also a rich source of antioxidants and naturally occurring nitrates, shown to improve blood flow to the brain, muscles, and heart.

Lucian nodded at the food. "Fuel for the day."

Evan sat down and sunk his spoon into a bowl of oatmeal. Calories during high-intensity training would be functional now. It was all about energy. He watched as Lucian pulled a bottle of Jim Beam rye from a drawer and then filled his flask carefully. Was he going to bring up the fact that Lucian was an alcoholic? No, some things were too sensitive.

Evan took a sip of beetroot juice, cringing from the sourness. "So you trained McKnight..."

Lucian looked at Evan out of the corner of his eye.

"I came here the day after I caught him in bed with my girlfriend. He's no superior man, that's for sure."

Lucian squeezed his flask. "You could be, though."

Evan finished eating and rifled through his duffel bag. He pulled out an iPod and held it just long enough for Lucian to knock it to the floor. "This isn't soccer practice," Lucian said. "You can't listen to music in a race like this."

Evan pulled out a heart rate monitor. "What about this?"

Lucian shook his head. "Too many people depend on gadgets. You will learn to listen to your body and to trust your instincts." He walked into the kitchen and retuned with a small espresso cup. "Two shots of espresso. Helps endurance."

Caffeine was proven to improve endurance during exercise, a known "ergogenic," an external influence that enhanced performance in high-intensity exercise. But Evan refused. "No thanks."

Lucian looked impressed. "Confucius would be proud." He tipped the espresso cup back and drank it with one gulp. "To Black Pond."

* * *

6:30 AM. A thin fog in the olive grove as Lucian led Evan to the pond. "Black Pond isn't that big," Lucian said, "but it's two miles around the perimeter, which is good enough for training."

Lucian tossed Evan an Aqua Sphere wetsuit. It took Evan almost ten minutes to get the ultra-tight-fitting suit over his singlet and up to his neck. He used the zipper at his lower back to seal the suit. Then Lucian handed Evan a pair of TYR swim goggles. Evan affixed them to his head as Lucian looked across the calm water. "My training philosophy is very simple: over the next twelve months we're going to make your workouts so miserable that by the time you get to Greece, it's going to seem like a walk in the park."

Evan couldn't help finding that a little intimidating. "Pain is my friend, that sorta thing?"

"Aches, pains, cramps, blisters, even injury… you'll learn to remove your judgment of 'pain' sensations, until hopefully you become immune to them." He grinned. "Now get in the water. It's two miles around the perimeter; I want at least one lap."

The suit provided some warmth, but the water was frigid and took Evan's breath away. He waded in waist deep, so that his palms skimmed the surface. He dove in head first and assumed a freestyle swim stroke, circling his arms forward, alternating arms. It was less than a minute before he began thrashing and popped his head out of the water, gasping for air.

Lucian shook his head from the beach.

Almost two hours later Evan finished the 2-mile swim. Lucian led Evan back to the house for a "second breakfast" that included an electrolyte replacement drink, Greek yogurt, blueberries, and granola. Then Lucian led Evan to his garage and presented a gorgeous triathlon bicycle. "This is a Specialized Shiv Expert," Lucian said. "It's one of the best triathlon bikes on the market. It's usually just called the 'Shiv.'"

Lucian asked Evan to sit on the bike and then adjusted settings to fit his body. He changed the saddle height, stance width, and the position of the handlebars. The bike had a built-in hydration system, which Lucian tightened with a screwdriver. He showed Evan how to pump the tires, lube the chain, and demonstrated several riding positions for optimal performance. In a small bag attached to the bike frame, he stuffed a few GU Energy Gels—packets that provided an optimal blend of carbohydrates, amino acids, electrolytes, and vitamins, perfect for endurance exercise. Finally, Lucian handed Evan a bike helmet and bike shoes. "This is a low-profile Uvex helmet, and these shoes are the best, from a French company called Mavic."

At 9:15 AM, Evan took off on a three-hour bike ride around Mather Gorge. The route ran along steep cliffs that dropped off into a majestic gorge. Sometimes, when the route flattened out, he would hug the Potomac and feel the spray of the rapids.

Lucian followed behind in his old, beat-up Volkswagen, instructing Evan on when to sip water or Gatorade. He also barked orders: "Back straight," "elbows in," and "keep your cadence high… works your cardiovascular system, saves your legs." Lucian would look at his watch and say, "Have a gel."

It was about 2 PM when Evan finished, and he was wrecked. But training wasn't over, apparently. Lucian led Evan into his basement to a treadmill. Evan laced-up his Brooks running shoes and hopped on.

"These are called mile repeats," Lucian said, increasing the treadmill's speed to 8.5 miles per hour. "This is about a seven-minute mile pace. Because it's your first day, we'll only run three miles, with one-minute breaks in between." Five minutes into the run, Evan was overcome with nausea, the color of his face turned ashen. He tasted vomit in the back of his throat. Lucian grabbed a bucket and Evan threw up violently. "Get it out, and reset," Lucian said, holding Evan's arm, inching him back toward the treadmill. "We'll get those calories back later."

Lucian had another meal ready an hour later, which consisted of a large egg scrambled with spinach and mushrooms and two large bowls of watermelon. Lucian added a dissolvable endurance powder called Perpetuem to a glass of water. He stirred it, and handed it to Evan. Like the Gu Gels, the blend provided consistent energy as well as helped improve fat utilization, and buffered lactic acid build up to prevent muscle fatigue. Evan grabbed the glass. He took a deep breath and chugged it in four gulps.

While they ate lunch, Lucian pulled out a map of Greece with the course traced onto it. Lucian started with the swim. "It's saltwater swimming, and the water will likely be choppy. You'll have to avoid rip currents. There will be jelly fish all around, which you can get tangled up in." Lucian traced his finger south along the bike portion of the race, and then west from Sparta to Athens.

The running portion of the race ends just East of Athens on Egaleo Mountain, about 1,539 feet high. It'll be a pain in the ass after 560 miles of cycling."

It was around 7:30 PM when Lucian and Evan had dinner. Lucian made a salad with kale, avocado, blueberries, fennel, and olive oil as well as two large chicken breasts. Evan ate wildly, barely taking a breath between bites. But even his intense hunger couldn't distract Evan from the pain all over. Every muscle in his body wailed.

"What if I can't do this, Lucian?" Evan asked.

"You can't," Lucian said, setting his fork down. "Not as you are now."

The wine had gotten to Lucian, but he appeared lucid, and eager to impart some hard-earned wisdom, it seemed. *In vino veritas…* in wine there is truth.

Lucian continued. "The person you are now will not be the same person you are at the end of our training. You will change. Most people think they are a finished product. They believe they stop changing at some point. But the truth is that we are in a constant state of flux. Our desires, our taste in music, people, all of these change. We cringe over things we said or did years ago, because we are almost not the same person. The human mind is ever-changing, endlessly creative, dark as it is bright, but it is fundamentally unfixed. You must look at yourself as a work in progress. See yourself as a sculptor. Chisel away at yourself, shaving parts off, smoothing out others. If you don't see yourself as you want to be, keep sculpting until you become what you have envisioned."

Twenty-Seven

Paramythia, Greece

Evan had only gotten four hours of sleep, but it was time to get back on the bike. He rolled over and shut his eyes, still troubled by his decision to take the shortcut. Lucian would often speak of the Greek philosophers. Plato wrote that Socrates was guided by a *daimon*, a guardian angel. Socrates said his daimon spoke a language with just one word: *No*. If Socrates were tempted to do wrong, he'd hear that word. Evan wondered if everyone had a daimon. Did McKnight… Dana? Perhaps they had found a way to silence them, even execute them. When Gardner recommended the shortcut, Evan had definitely heard his "daimon." But he had ignored it.

The problem with cheating was conscience. Even if no one else knew what you did, *you* still knew. Lucian talked about Confucius' "superior man." He had made Evan read the *Analects*, a collection of sayings from Confucius. Lucian told Evan that it was a roadmap for becoming a *junzi*, meaning gentleman, and eventually a virtuous, "superior" man. According to the *Analects*, *'de,'* or moral character, wasn't innate. Morality was a thing to be cultivated. According to Lucian, giving up performance enhancers in college and catching that soccer ball had both been the "right" thing for Evan to do. A starting point at least. But Evan couldn't shake the feeling that taking the shortcut had compromised him again. He felt no different than McKnight, than his old self.

Evan packed up his tent, and handed it to Tim. "Why don't you drive ahead?" Evan said, "I'm going to go to the bathroom behind those rocks." As

Evan began urinating, he closed his eyes and let his head fall back. The camp was quiet. Most of the athletes had either started their rides toward Sparta, or were still sleeping. A few were sitting around a small fire, eating quickly. Evan heard whispering voices. He zipped up his pants and tip-toed around a corner to see a tent, which looked deliberately set-up away from camp. Evan saw silhouettes of people inside. He scooted closer, hunched over. The voices were low, but he could just make out the words.

A voice asked, "Did Masterson give you a drug test last night?"

The second person said, "Yep, my numbers were perfect."

Numbers? Evan thought.

"Let's do this quickly," the man continued, "I've got a long day on the bike."

Evan saw the man open a bag and fiddle with some small instruments on the tent's floor. He moved in close to the other man. "This will sting a little."

"Just do it." He looked away, sticking out his arm. Still looking away, he asked, "Is this blood from my Mount Olympus rides?"

"Liquid gold."

A small bag was lifted, and Evan knew immediately that he was witnessing a blood transfusion. The "numbers" had to be a reference to Masterson's performance enhancement test. Apparently, the athlete had passed.

Blood doping worked by withdrawing several units of blood from the body a few weeks before competition. The blood was then centrifuged to separate red blood cells from other blood cells and components. Plasma was returned to the athlete, but the red blood cells were refrigerated or frozen. A few weeks before a competition, or even during a competition, the RBCs were returned to the athlete's blood. Because red blood cells carried oxygen, an injection of them increased the athlete's oxygen-carrying capacity, enhancing the cardio-vascular system, creating a more efficient endurance athlete. Since the blood was their own, there were no concerns about immune rejection. Typically, the blood was withdrawn after having lived and trained at high-altitude, which stimulated the body to overproduce RBCs.

Evan thought for a moment: the athlete asked if the blood was from Mount Olympus rides; could it be…

Someone unzipped the tent.

Evan scurried behind a rock as the man stepped out and scanned the area. The man strolled by him and through the center of camp. Evan peered around the rock—he didn't recognize him. The other man stepped from the tent and into the sunlight. Evan recognized him right away.

It was Julius.

Evan walked into view, and his confusion must have shown on his face.

Julius's jaw dropped. "Evan…?" his voice trailed. "How long have you—?"

"Long enough." Confusion gave way to disappointment. "That talk about purity."

"All of Greece is counting on me. Do you have any idea what kind of pressure I'm under? I'm forty-six years old. I do what I *have to do* to compete."

"I thought you were different."

Julius became angry. "Says the guy who took a fifty-mile shortcut. Who are you to pass judgment?"

Evan didn't know what to say.

Julius flexed his jaw. "Face it: you, me, McKnight… we're all cut from the same cloth."

Julius was right. Evan was a hypocrite. He had cheated. But maybe there was something he could do. He turned toward camp and began walking away, a determined expression on his face.

Julius snatched his shoulder, spinning Evan like a top. "Where the hell are you going?" He squinted. "Are you going to tell on me?"

Evan knocked Julius's hand away and then locked eyes with a race official in a red vest.

"Look, look, what I did was disgraceful, I know."

Evan kept walking as Julius hurried to keep up alongside him.

"I'm not proud of it. But don't do this." He sounded afraid. "*Please.*"

Evan reached the race official, an older man staring at a clipboard. "Can I help you?" he asked, adjusting his glasses.

Evan took a breath. "I'd like to report a violation. I cheated."

"Excuse me?" the official said. Julius looked incredulous.

Evan gulped, but stayed composed. "Earlier this morning, I took a short-cut that cut fifty miles off the route."

The official squinted, obviously trying to confirm if Evan was serious. "You realize that is a serious offense."

"I do."

"And did anyone else take this shortcut with you?"

Evan didn't miss a beat. "No, just me."

The official bit his lip and then walked toward a small group. They glanced at Evan as they talked.

Julius started to speak, but Evan interrupted him. "Go."

Julius was solemn. "No one had to know."

Evan watched the officials point to a thin pamphlet and talk rapidly. "I could have gotten away with it, you're right." He stared at the ground. "You know I've played sports all my life, and coaches have always shoved the same winning-at-all-costs philosophy down my throat." He paused. "But what good would winning be if I couldn't look at myself in the mirror afterwards?"

Julius said nothing, but looked pensive. Evan patted the big man on the shoulder. "Good luck, Julius."

Julius grimaced and then meandered away, his head low with dishonor. Evan knew he would be disqualified, but at least he could live with himself.

Twenty-Eight

It had been a week of training and Evan hadn't improved as a swimmer, runner, or biker. He had swum before, but never competitively, not to Lucian's standards. According to Lucian, Evan's form was all wrong. His legs hung too low in the water, creating drag; his head was too high with each breath; and he didn't swim straight, moving in a zig-zag through the water. A big part of the problem was that Evan simply fatigued so fast. He wasn't an endurance athlete. Soccer required short bursts of speed and skill, repeated over forty-five minutes at a time, whereas long-distance running demanded sustained activity over much longer periods. As a natural sprinter, Evan had more fast twitch muscle fibers than slow, and was at a genetically disadvantage for endurance sports. He would have to work harder.

Lucian didn't participate in training sessions. Rather, he would bark orders and then retreat to the olive grove where he would stroll and think. Sometimes he would retreat into the house to meditate. Meditation, it turned out, was a crucial part of Lucian's training regime. Every morning in Lucian's library, Evan participated in what Lucian called "mindfulness training."

"Almost all elite athletes will tell you that they operate from a quiet center," Lucian said. "Without this center, there's tension in the body. Find this center and act from it. But just as an athlete must be aware of his body, he must keep a closer watch over his mind."

Lucian asked Evan to sit cross-legged on a round cushion. "Back straight, don't slump. Examine your body, and suspend your judgment of any sensations or feelings. Notice thoughts. Then let him drift away."

Evan found meditation enormously difficult at first. It was as much of a mental challenge as the rest of the training was a physical challenge. The moment he closed his eyes, thoughts overwhelmed him.

Worse, Lucian apparently could tell when Evan's thoughts had hijacked his consciousness. "Picture each thought as if it were a wrapped present coming down a conveyor belt. Let the conveyor belt bring the present toward you, inspect it briefly, and then let it be carried away."

In his mind's eye, Evan played back the night he interrupted Dana and McKnight. The thought pulled him out of the present. He was lost, ripped from the now.

Lucian tapped Evan on the shoulder. "Where'd you go?"

"I was thinking," Evan said, cracking open his eyes. "I'm not good at this."

"Calming the mind is hard, but with practice, you'll learn. You will learn to detach from your thoughts. The mind is a powerful instrument, Evan, but you must become its master. Most people let the instrument control them."

"So, am I supposed to never have a thought?"

"The problem isn't our thoughts; every day we have thousands. The problem is that we let our thoughts hook us and take us for a ride." Lucian's eyebrows rose. "Bet you're pretty mad at McKnight and your boss, right?"

Evan narrowed his eyes.

"I bet thinking about them together gets you all riled up?"

He clenched his fists.

"Emotions are part of being human. If you feel sad, be sad. If you feel angry, be angry. But learn to detach. Notice when a thought has its hook in you and gracefully let it go."

Evan closed his eyes and took a deep breath. He visualized the number one as he took a slow, deliberate breath. The goal was to count to ten without being distracted by a thought. At number three, Evan found himself thinking about Dana, the day she'd distracted him while Tim was in the hypobaric chamber. He restarted the count.

After maybe fifteen meditation sessions, it started to get easier to "stay in the moment." Evan's mind became stiller. Thoughts came with less frequency, and when they did, he could release them with greater ease. He found that a mental calmness started to carry over into daily life. His mind used to wander while running and biking, but after several weeks of meditation, he could stay focused on the activity, and could keep a close watch on his body and its performance.

Evan was impressed with Lucian's knowledge of Eastern and Western philosophies. The man's bookshelves were filled with classic literature, such as the *Iliad* and the *Odyssey* by the epic poet Homer, *Meditations* by the Roman emperor and Stoic philosopher Marcus Aurelius, *The Republic* by Plato, and works by Aristotle, who penned philosophical works such as *Ethics*, *Poetics* and *Politics*.

During quiet evenings, Evan would read with Lucian in his library, and meditate on the wisdom from these ancient books. It was cathartic to read from these great thinkers each night. While their profound thoughts reminded him of Evan of his own perceived virtues, they also brought him face-to-face with his mistakes, the events in his life that he wished he could take back. He enjoyed the French philosopher Michel de Montaigne and his magnum opus, *Essays*. In it, Montaigne wrote, "The greatest thing in the world is to know how to belong to oneself." Evan wished that he could achieve that. There would be peace in that moment. He also wished it for his teacher, who obviously hadn't come to terms with his own demons. Lucian continued to drink too much, even as he read.

Evan and Lucian were in the library one night when Lucian pulled a book off the bookshelf called *The Art of Dramatic Writing*. He flipped to the foreword, entitled "The Importance of Being Important." He said, "This is a book for playwrights, but it provides insight into human behavior, especially someone like Jack McKnight." Lucian pointed to a chair. "Please, sit. I want to read you the foreword."

Evan sat and Lucian leaned against the fireplace mantle. Holding the book in his hand, he said, "This is a parable, a story set in Ancient Greece. One night in Athens, a statue of Zeus was found destroyed in a temple. It caused uproar among the people, as they feared the gods would punish them because of the desecration. People stormed the streets, demanding that the criminal show himself. He didn't. The next week, another statue was found ruined. Guards were posted everywhere in an attempt to catch the criminal. Eventually, the hunt was successful and the criminal was caught. I will read directly from the book here:

"The criminal was asked, 'Do you know what fate awaits you?'

'Yes,' he answered, almost cheerfully. 'Death.'

'Aren't you afraid to die?'

'Yes, I am.'

'Then why did you commit a crime which you knew was punishable by death?'

The man swallowed hard and then answered. 'I am nobody. All my life I've been a nobody. I've never done anything to distinguish myself and I knew I never would. I wanted to do something to make people notice me... and remember me.'

After a moment's silence, he added, 'Only those people die who are forgotten. I feel death is a small price to pay for immortality!'"

Lucian closed the book. "All of Jack McKnight's conquests, his mountaineering and athletic adventures and financial accomplishments, they're all but ways to feel important, to get attention, to *feel outstanding*."

"He's taken it pretty far with the myths of Achilles," Evan said.

"He read about Achilles in this library." Lucian walked to the bookshelf and grabbed the *Iliad*. "Achilles was a great warrior in Homer's *Iliad*. The quintessential hero. For those who subscribe to Homeric epics like this, dying without fame is a disaster. Like Achilles, McKnight needs to be remembered. More than anything, he craves immortality."

"That's what his bracelet is all about?"

Lucian's face turned red with anger. "*That bracelet* was in my family for four generations." He faced the fireplace. "McKnight stole it." He lowered his head. "He stole more than that when he crushed my campaign with that Masterson."

"So, that's what happened," Evan said, finally understanding.

"I thought if I could make the game pure by speaking out, I could get something back. I thought I could redeem myself. But McKnight used his wealth and power to crush me."

"So McKnight wants to live forever?" Evan asked. He could understand the desire. After all, he'd been furious when Weng had claimed Evan's work as his own.

"And he will do anything to make sure that he is remembered," Lucian said. "He will lie, steal, and cheat."

Evan had to ask the next question. "In this Dramatic Writing book, what happens if we don't get attention? What happens if we don't feel important? Or if we think we'll be forgotten?"

Lucian continued reading from the foreword: "If we can't create something useful or beautiful, we shall certainly create something else... *trouble*."

Twenty-Nine

Paramythia, Greece

To Evan's amazement, the race officials didn't disqualify him from the race. But they did give him a one-hour time penalty, ordering him to wait in Paramythia as the rest of the athletes mounted their bikes and rode off ahead of him. Evan was grateful that the officials had been lenient, but an hour was a death sentence at this stage of a race like the *Aletheia*. No amount of effort could make up such a deficit. But he would try.

When he got back on his bike, it was as if he had been shot out of a cannon. He thought if he could somehow reach Sparta before midnight, he would be in decent shape. He would need to average a speed of about 30 miles per hour, which would demand a tremendous amount of effort and focus. He decided he wouldn't sleep in Sparta, which many athletes were planning to do before the 131-mile run. It would mean running while already exhausted. Evan knew he would have to push himself harder than he had ever pushed himself. He would have to reach his limits, and then push past them.

As a limits physiologist, Evan was aware of the fact the environmental conditions weren't favorable for maximum intensity work. It was 9:45 am, but it was still 84 degrees Fahrenheit and the sun was scorching. He would need to monitor his hydration closely. In such hot and humid conditions, he would require much more water than normal. Heat exhaustion and heat stroke were real threats.

Steering his bike with one hand, Evan took massive gulps of water from his water bottle. The western coast of Greece was gorgeous. While he kept his head low for aerodynamics, he looked around and enjoyed the epic mountains that shot from the ground and ended in needle-like rock pillars. Cliffside monasteries towered over the land like tiny mountain kingdoms. The dwellings along the side of the road seemed free from the worries of modern life. These tiny mountain villages did, indeed, seem "pure" as Julius said. Evan pumped his legs, hurrying him along the coastal roads.

Evan sped through villages, his head rocking left and right with each piston-like movement of his legs. His lower body burned from the effort, but he ignored the pain as it came in waves. For the first part of his ride, he was alone, then, one-by-one, he started to overtake competitors. He kept his gaze forward as he blew past them. They all looked to be suffering. He shot across a stone bridge, passing two more athletes. He maintained a blistering pace as he entered into Preveza, a small Greek town at the mouth of the Ambracian Gulf. As he cut through the town's streets and alleys, he passed taverns and bustling cafes. In the background were the blue waters of the Ionian Sea and, further off, the Thesprotian Mountains.

Evan passed through the town's port, filled with yachts, and then came upon a group of race volunteers who were funneling athletes into the Aktio–Preveza Undersea Tunnel, a passageway connecting Preveza to Epirus that allowed gulf-crossings without having to take a ferry. For once, the route was closed. The one-mile tunnel had been reserved for racers only. The hot sun disappeared as Evan entered the tunnel, and an eerie yellow light took its place.

Thirty

Greenway, Virginia

It had been two months of training, and Evan couldn't stand the inside of Lucian's weight room anymore. It wasn't the musty smell or the dim lighting; it was simply that the space represented pain and failure. Evan had never worked his body so hard. Gym workouts with Lucian were circuits containing a mixture of weight lifting followed by high-intensity plyometric exercises. Even breaks were "working breaks" that meant keep moving. One would involve running at eight miles per hour for one minute on the treadmill; others might be kettle bell swings, or dumbbell cleans.

It was grueling and sometimes Evan felt like he wasn't making progress, but he did look different in the mirror. The flab around his waist was shrinking. His chest, arms, and legs were hardening. He could go a little longer and harder during aerobic exercises. It was good to feel like an athlete again, however awful it felt during the actual training.

Every day Lucian pushed Evan to the edge of his abilities. If Evan ran a 5K in 30 minutes, Lucian demanded he complete the next in 27 minutes. There were moments when Evan thought he might be able to do well in the *Aletheia*, but these hopes were dashed whenever he reminded himself of the Nan Airs' power. He had read that McKnight had bought a house near the Oracle of Delphi, which seemed typical given McKnight's obsession with mythological places, characters, and places. One newspaper had written that McKnight had been studying the triathlon's route, even cycling portions of it. First-hand knowledge of the course would give him an advantage.

It was around this time, several months into training, that the prospect of competing with McKnight and Luke began to seem impossible. It was too daunting. The training had gotten increasingly punishing. The early morning jogs, the double and triple sessions in the gym. The Spartan-like nutritional regimen. He felt like Sisyphus, continually rolling a boulder up a hill only to watch it roll back again and again. It was in this moment of weakness when he used Lucian's home phone to call Coach Helmsley.

"Coach," Evan said.

Coach Helmsley was cheerful. "Evan, hey man! It's good to hear from you. Did you end up meeting up with Lucian? Is he kicking your butt or what?"

"I'm training with him, yeah." Evan got to the point. "Coach, I've decided that I can't do this on my own. I think I need help... something extra."

"Something extra like what you used in college?"

"Yeah."

"You know I don't support that anymore."

"You know I don't either." But he needed it right then. There was no other way.

Helmsley still didn't give in. "Have you thought about this? Really thought about it? Those anti-doping guys… if they catch you..."

"*I'm sure*," Evan said.

Helmsley breathed heavily into the phone. "I still have that guy's number. I guess I could give him a call. Evan, if you go down this road again—"

That was when Evan locked eyes with Lucian, standing motionless in the hall just a few feet away. Evan didn't move. What was Lucian going to do? Surely he'd throw him out of his house. Or maybe he'd just punish him with extra workouts. But Lucian did something unexpected. He turned around, walked into his room, and closed the door. Evan could only characterize Lucian's expression as compassionate, perhaps because Evan looked guilty, even ashamed, perhaps because Lucian knew the impulse to seek out an edge.

It was a moment of weakness for Evan, a step backward. But he hadn't crossed the line. He'd only put his toe to it. And now he would step back.

"I've got to go, Coach. Sorry I called."

Evan slowly hung up the phone, and remembered Lucian's words in the kitchen: "Moral progress starts with the shame in one's inconsistency." He hadn't lived up to Lucian's code of conduct, but he had felt shame in being inconsistent. Evan knew they would never talk about what happened. Evan decided to wake up the next morning and try to be better.

Thirty-One

Central Greece

Evan exited the Aktio–Preveza Undersea Tunnel at full speed, and was met by a thick blanket of hot, heavy air. It must have been 95 degrees, and with the high humidity, sweat evaporation was practically nonexistent, making it difficult for Evan's body to cool. His skin began to flush, and a headache set in. He couldn't be far from heat exhaustion. He used his water bottle to spray water on his face. He began to feel dizzy, and realized he hadn't urinated in a long time. That was worrying too, an early sign of dehydration. Evan drank more water, but still felt hot and lethargic. Cramps set in next, first in his calves and then his feet. When a foot cramped, he was forced to stop pedaling, click his bike shoe out of its toe hook, and lift his leg in the air while the cramp took its course.

The symptoms continued to worsen. When he felt his heart rate become erratic and started to feel nauseous, he knew that the heat stroke was getting worse. If he didn't get medical help, his high core temperature could damage his brain and internal organs. If not treated, it could even cause death.

He saw a rider ahead. He pedaled to them, hoping they could help. He realized it was Isabella. Evan came up alongside her and tried to say something, but the words came out in a jumble.

"Evan," Isabella said, happily. But her face quickly dropped when she recognized the emergency. "Oh no, are you okay?"

Evan hung his head low. "No."

He couldn't manage more than that. He felt dizzy and light-headed. His headache was throbbing. He began to feel so weak that he thought he might tip off the bike.

Isabella waved her arms at her support car. The driver pulled the car up alongside her. "Get the cold bandages and put some ice and water in a bucket."

Evan didn't have the strength to thank her. Instead, he tumbled off his bike. They'd slowed by then, but he still hit the pavement hard, scuffing his knees and cutting the palm of his hand. Isabella leapt off her bike and rushed to his side.

"Your skin's too hot," she said. "Let's get to the shade."

She helped Evan crawl across the hot pavement toward a tree across the road. Her support man ran over with a medical kit and a bottle of water. He handed it to her and then ran back to the car's trunk.

"The shade will help cool you." Isabella poured water on Evan's face and down the back of his neck. She poured some into his mouth. Her support man returned with a bucket of water. He dumped three large bags of ice into it and then dunked long bandages in the water. Isabella took one. "Lift up your arm." She placed a wet bandage underneath both of Evan's armpits. She wrapped another around his neck, and put one on his forehead and one at his groin. She was placing the cold bandages in areas rich in blood vessels close to the skin. The idea was that the cooled blood would travel through the body, cooling internal organs and helping to bring his core body temperature back into safe limits. Evan felt it working. After five minutes, his skin was no longer bright red and the dizziness had lifted. Life was returning.

"There you go," Isabella said, tipping chilled water into Evan's mouth. She gave him a peanut butter and jelly sandwich while she ate Ritz crackers and butter. Evan gulped too much water and began coughing. He wiped water from his chin. "Thank you."

"Don't mention it." She gave him more water. "You have to be careful pushing it that hard in this heat." She grinned. "Must be that late start you got."

Evan still felt woozy, but he gave her an inquisitive look. "What do you mean?"

"So you took a shortcut…" she said, shrugging her shoulders. "People have done worse things."

Evan looked sheepish. He hadn't wanted her to know.

"You confessed to it, so all is good." She placed a hand underneath his chin and brought his eyes to hers. "I guess that's why you were so shy around the fire last night."

Evan smiled slightly. "We've still got a race to finish."

Isabella bit her lip playfully. She turned to her support man. "How far are the others ahead of us, Georgio?"

The man ran a hand through his hair. "You guys are in ninth and tenth right now. But you can ride fast on the Peloponnese peninsula to make up time."

Evan felt renewed from the ice and cold water. "You ready to do this?"

She grinned. "I'll race you to Sparta."

The two sprinted to their bikes and sped off at breakneck speed.

Thirty-Two

Greenway, Virginia

Evan slid his head underneath the barbell on the bench press. Lucian stood above him, spotting; he placed his hands under the barbell. "One more set on the bench. I want at least one repetition at 265."

That was ten pounds more than Evan's previous best. Evan took a deep breath and placed his hands on the barbell. He blew out air and then hoisted the barbell up over his chest. He inhaled deeply and lowered the weight, letting the barbell meet his chest. He blew out a breath, and pressed the barbell hard. But the barbell stayed on his chest, barely budging. Holding his breath, he pressed harder, arching his back up off the bench. The barbell moved an inch and then a few more. Evan's face turned red as he pushed harder. His hands shook, arms wobbled. Not knowing what else to do, Evan arched his lower back high and used the power from his legs to lift the weight higher, until he swung the barbell backward and onto the hooks. He slumped down, spent.

Lucian walked away, irritated.

"That's a new max." Evan sat up, confused. "What's wrong with you?"

"It doesn't count. You used your back and legs."

"Oh, c'mon, man. Would you give me a break for once?"

Lucian turned, looking fierce. "It's not just what you do; it's how you do it. An athlete's character is more important than his triumphs."

Evan was sick of the talk about virtue and morality. "People get away with little cheats every day. Anyway, I tried 'doing the right thing,' and I lost."

"And now you think you need to cheat to get ahead, is that it?"

Evan said nothing.

"If you can't do an exercise the right way, you can't do it at all." Lucian snatched the flask from his back pocket and walked away.

Evan was furious. "You're pointing the finger at me!" He looked at the flask in Lucian's hand. "You're a drunk, what do you have to feel good about?" Evan pointed to the bench. "Why don't you put that flask down and let's see how honorable and strong you are."

Lucian was still for a moment, and then he marched past Evan to the bench. Evan watched him remove the ten-pound weights from the barbell and replace them with two 45-pound weights. The barbell held 315 pounds. Evan suddenly became concerned for the old man. Lucian wouldn't be able to bench that weight. Evan approached the bench, intending to talk him out of it when Lucian raised his hand.

"You can see just fine from where you are."

Lucian slid underneath the barbell, and closed his eyes. A deep calm seemed to come over him. Then Lucian's eyes snapped open and his face contorted with aggression. He sucked in air, and lifted the barbell off the hooks. Evan imagined the horrific possibilities—Lucian dropping the weight, crushing his chest; letting the barbell roll back onto his neck, strangling him. At best, it might tip to the side, toppling the bench system over. None of those scenarios happened, however. Instead, Lucian lowered the barbell, touched it to his chest and pressed it up and down five times, and then placed the barbell back onto the hooks. It was an impressive performance, but Lucian wasn't finished. Saying nothing, Lucian passed Evan and went upstairs. He returned with an egg.

Evan had a puzzled look on his face.

"Take this from me."

Evan could tell Lucian was serious. "You want me to take that egg from you?"

Lucian split his legs wide, readying himself.

Evan squinted, but he was still annoyed, and relished the opportunity to engage Lucian hand-to-hand. He ran at Lucian, crashed his shoulder into him and wrapped his hands around his tight fist. He tried to get his fingers under Lucian's, but the man's grip was shockingly strong. Evan struggled for a couple of minutes or so before giving up, out of breath and defeated.

Lucian set the egg on a table. It should have been crushed within Lucian's fist, but instead it sat undamaged. Lucian wasn't done though. He straightened his back and held out his hand with his thumb up and fingers spread.

"If you can bend my little finger at all," he said, "we will take the rest of the day off."

Evan pounced, ripping at Lucian's fingers. But his fingers stayed perfectly straight, locked in an open position. Evan admitted defeat again.

Lucian walked back to the bench and began removing the weight with a determined look on his face. "You're going to do this next set *clean*." Evan was approaching the bench when Lucian's doorbell rang on the first floor. Lucian never had visitors. Evan followed him upstairs. Lucian swung open the door and staring back at him was a tall, heavyset man in a business suit. He had dark, receding hair and wore tortoise shell glasses.

"Morning, Lucian," the man said with a smirk.

Lucian's nostrils flared as he glared at the man. "What the *hell* are you doing here?"

"I'm looking for Evan Galloway," the man said, nonchalantly. "He's competing in the *Aletheia* next summer."

"I don't know how you found my house, but you can un-find it." Lucian began closing the door.

The man stuck his foot out, stopping the door from closing. He looked over at Evan. "My name is Frank Masterson. Head of the Advisory panel for the World Doping Agency-"

Lucian cut him off. "Get the hell off of my property."

"I'm afraid I can't leave until Mr. Galloway has performed a mandatory drug test. It's required of all athletes participating in the race."

"Let's just get this over with?" Evan suggested. He had agreed to be tested when he'd signed up for the race. He couldn't turn Masterson away if he wanted to compete.

Baring his teeth, Lucian swept his hand out "inviting" Masterson inside. It was all business from there. Masterson pulled a plastic cup from his bag and handed it to Evan. Evan walked to the bathroom and filled the cup with urine.

"Well, I guess that'll be all," Lucian said. He didn't bother trying to hide his dislike for the man. "Thanks for stopping by."

Masterson raised a finger, not finished, it seemed. "Just have to perform a quick blood test. *Then* I'll be done."

Lucian mumbled something under his breath as Evan sat down at the dining room table. Masterson removed a small instrument from a kit. "Now you'll feel a little pressure."

He pricked Evan's finger with a needle, drawing a drop of blood.

As the machine calibrated, Lucian scowled at Masterson. "I can't believe you can just sit there, after everything you and McKnight did to me."

"Everything *we* did?" He shot Evan a look of amusement. "You probably think this guy's some kind of guru, I bet? Some great athlete?" Lucian was fuming as he continued. "This man used performance-enhancing drugs for his entire athletic career, made people believe in him, gave them hope. But it was all a lie. So after he got banned from sports for life, I was supposed to believe his anti-doping campaign?"

Lucian pointed a finger at him. "I was trying to make it—"

"Right?" Masterson scoffed. "There's no coming back from what you did. No redemption. You lied to fans, to officials like me. But, most of all, to yourself. You destroyed those who got in your way, put them down like weak dogs. You think I was going to believe you were rehabilitated? Once a cheat, always a cheat."

Lucian hung his head low. "You're wrong."

Masterson gathered his materials and packed his bag. "I wouldn't listen to this guy, Evan. He'll only bring you down." He gave Lucian a smirk. "I'd say I'd see you at the race next summer, but—wait, that's right—you can't set foot in an Olympic stadium."

Lucian rushed Masterson and grabbed him by the collar. "I ought to kick your ass."

He raised his fist to punch him, but Evan grabbed Lucian's arm, stopping him before he could land a blow.

"Leave us alone," Evan said.

"You'd better stay on the straight and narrow," Masterson said. "One slip up, and it's game over for you."

Evan closed the door and watched Lucian hustle for his flask on the counter. Lucian screwed the cap off his flask and went to take a sip. Just before he did it, he looked back at Evan. He stopped, the lid pressed to his lips. Lucian looked out the window and then screwed the cap back on tight.

Thirty-Three

Central Greece

McKnight adjusted his eye patch and looked down the long stretch of road below him. Under his feet was a tunnel just wide enough for a car, a passageway through the massive rock formation on which McKnight stood. The slope was steep and covered in rocks of varying sizes, from tiny pebbles to near boulders, but all of it was loose and unstable. McKnight guessed that kicking one or two large rocks would likely cause the whole hill to slide away in an avalanche. The ground would tumble off the overhang and rain down on whoever was unlucky enough to be at the tunnel's entrance. The newspapers would call it a "natural" disaster. No one would be able to trace it back to him.

Even after six painkillers, his eye still throbbed, and the stab wound to his leg was a constant source of excruciating pain. The wound's appearance had worsened in the hours since the fight, becoming black and hard. Pedaling with a defective leg had taken tremendous willpower, and running 131 miles was going to take Herculean strength. But he had led expeditions through Antarctica and climbed the Nose route on El Capitan in under two hours—a little fresh wound wasn't going to rob him of his glory.

Plus, he had Nan Airs, a miracle of science. He thought people were probably looking for Masterson by now. McKnight didn't care. He'd be out of the country by the time the investigation got underway.

Once McKnight started the avalanche, the falling cliff face would undoubtedly crush whoever was below. He saw a rider in the distance. He stood up and positioned his foot to start the landslide, but he paused and then pulled back when he noticed it was Luke. To McKnight's astonishment, Luke wasn't the competitor he needed to worry about. McKnight had competed in many triathlons with Luke, and while he was a fine competitor, he didn't have his brother's killer steely determination and resolve. McKnight had seen Luke fold at important moments during races. Evan was racing naturally and yet he was somehow competing. McKnight had to admit, the kid had heart. But he was a threat to McKnight's victory, and he hadn't come this far to see some nerd from MIT win the day.

McKnight crouched down and watched Luke zip into the tunnel. He clutched his wounded leg as he stood up and looked down the road stretching out toward the horizon. He would wait for the perfect moment… for Evan.

Thirty-Four

Greenway, Virginia

Evan was 300 miles into a training bike ride when he reached the bottom of a steep hill. It would have been a grueling uphill climb at the best of times, but he had already swum six miles and run fifty. Driving beside Evan on the steepening road, Lucian was shouting advice, occasionally handing Evan a water bottle or an energy gel. The clouds were dark and fat with rain and a thick blanket of mist hugged the winding road.

Evan had felt strong on the bike for the past hour, immersed in the zone. Time had seemed to expand, so that the exercise felt enjoyable, even joyful. But in the last fifteen minutes, Evan's spirits had dampened. He thought about the day's nutrition, guessing he had consumed about 3,000 calories. It wasn't enough. Lucian was usually quick to hand him an energy gel when necessary, but he hadn't, and now Evan's legs felt heavy, his mind sluggish. The blissful, energized focus of the zone gave way to a crushing fatigue, a point at which his body's supply of glucose had been depleted. He was hitting the wall. He was physically and emotionally spent, but still he had to keep going. Somehow, he mustered the willpower to charge the hill for the climb ahead.

Evan's thoughts were erratic. It was remarkable to think that he could barely bike twenty miles before he had started training, and now he was ascending a small mountain *after* a 300-mile bike ride. Over the course of training, Lucian had registered Evan for many preparatory competitions, including 5Ks, sprint and Olympic-distance triathlons, half-marathons, and cycle races. Evan completed a half-ironman, performing the 1.2-mile swim in twenty-nine minutes, the 56-mile bike ride in two hours and eighteen minutes, and the 13.1-mile run in 5:25. Evan's time was fast, but he only finished eighth. It was encouraging that he could compete at such a high level, but he had read articles about McKnight winning endurance events handily.

Evan's performances were respectable, but still not good enough to beat McKnight or even his brother. To make up for it, Lucian pushed him beyond his limits in every training session. In Evan's first marathon, he ran his guts out and clocked a time of two hours and twenty-nine minutes, placing 33rd overall. In his first fifty-mile bike race, he came in 5th with a time of one hour and forty-eight minutes. Lucian pushed Evan harder and harder, and watched his diet closely. The running mileage was ramped up until Evan was doing about 115 miles per week, which increased to 150. Evan ran his second marathon in two hours and thirteen minutes, coming in 13th overall. Then he completed his next 50-miler in one hour and forty-one minutes to place 2nd overall.

Swimming was the most challenging activity for Evan, but Lucian was gifted in the water, and taught Evan mechanics for swimming with the least resistance to flow. Evan was able to iron out his bad habits, bit by bit. As his technique improved, he got faster in the water. Six months into training, he started winning Olympic-distance triathlons. Evan was shocked to see Lucian get in the water and swim with Evan sometimes. The best moment was when Evan beat Lucian in a swim around Black Pond. That day, Lucian emerged from the water while Evan stared at the sunset over the pond.

"You're ready," he said.

Evan was just happy to see him without a flask in his hand.

* * *

Evan was half-way through the hill climb and his muscles screamed. "I need an energy gel, Lucian."

Lucian ignored him and kept driving.

"I'm hitting the wall here," Evan said, "This isn't time for one of your lessons."

"When the soccer ball was crossed to you in that soccer game, the goal-keeper had fallen down injured. The net was open, and you could have easily kicked it in. You probably would have won the game. You probably would have played one day professionally. But you didn't shoot, did you?"

Evan couldn't hear him; all he could think about was the pain, the exhaustion. He wanted to stop, *needed* to stop. He feared his legs would revolt, and he would collapse, injuring himself or worse. The year of training had been all about learning how to manage suffering mentally. While he had learned how to manage pain, his body still showed the signs of training. Sometimes after a 50- or 100-mile run, he would have blisters the size of quarters, which Lucian would cut with a utility knife and then cover in alcohol and bacitracin. Running such long running distances made him especially prone to injuries caused by the repetitive motion, from toenails falling off to more serious injuries like plantar fasciitis, an inflammation of the heel, which Evan found caused intense pain while running, even walking.

A few weeks of ice and massage reduced the inflammation and discomfort, but the injury nagged and would occasionally return during particularly rigorous workouts. Evan also experienced Achilles tendinitis, a condition where the tendon that connects the back of the legs to the heel becomes inflamed. Luckily, Lucian identified it early and was able to offer strengthening exercises to help nurse it back to health before the tendon tore. While Evan's injuries healed, nothing seemed to heal *fully*. He learned how to train with pain as a constant.

* * *

Evan stood up on his pedals and churned his legs, but the road was a 20% gradient. He narrowed his eyes, his lower jaw slack. Between deep breaths, he closed his eyes briefly, as if he were trying to sleep in the moments where his lungs were empty. As his legs became weaker, they felt heavier and heavier. His body positions became excessive, causing the bike to rock back and forth.

Lucian's words about the infamous soccer game still rang in his head.

"You're suffering right now," Lucian continued. He drove close to Evan, and patted the side of the car. "Why don't you just reach out and grab the car and the pain will go away?"

Evan glanced at Lucian, confirming that he was serious. "No."

Lucian didn't let up. "Why not?"

"Because—"

"You think McKnight wouldn't grab hold, take a breather, get a little help… you think your brother wouldn't?"

Evan was breathing heavily. He forced himself to ignore the temptation even though it sat just inches away. The car could take the strain for a few hundred yards. He could recover. Not much, but enough to keep going. He didn't reach out.

Lucian looked over at him. "See Evan, in sport and in life, there are two types of people. There are those who pride themselves on their competitiveness, their ability to outwit, and think that winning isn't everything… it's the *only* thing. They are like Odysseus, Homer's famous hero in the *Iliad*. To Odysseus, any means justified a desired outcome. Were Odysseus presented with an unguarded net, he would have kicked the ball in faster that you can say Pelé." Lucian paused. "Some people, however, will not compromise their ethical principles. Such people are like Galahad, the purest of King Arthur's knights. For Galahad, virtue is non-negotiable. There's a code of conduct and they abide by it."

Evan listened as if from a long way away, lost in the effort and agony of the climb.

Lucian continued. "Sports have grown to favor an Odyssian ideal. People wonder if they have to cheat or deceive or bend the rules to win. People like McKnight will do anything to win, including using performance-enhancing drugs. The question is how *you* think they should be played, Evan."

Evan had thought about that question every day since the game. But the climb had turned Evan's mind to mush, so he couldn't answer properly, much less make a decision. Or maybe he still didn't know where he stood. He muttered. "I don't know… it didn't seem fair—"

"You have a conscience, Evan. When you were faced with a chance to take advantage of a situation, you chose honor."

Evan moved slowly on the bike, barely able to breathe. "Why does any of this matter?"

"Because you're still thinking about yourself, Evan. This isn't just about you. Modern sports favor an Odyssian attitude, but this is a chance to bring them back to where they should be. When I campaigned against doping, I was ignored, because I was viewed as too tainted. But your heart is pure, Evan. And maybe if you win *The Aletheian* clean, you can remind athletes of that ethos. It could spread into the Olympics, like a brushfire, reminding everyone that you don't have to cheat to win."

"You want me to be… a symbol?" Evan said.

"If you aren't, who will be?"

Evan said nothing, but found a surge of power in his legs. With renewed energy, he stood up on the pedals and pumped hard. The bike accelerated, shooting up the incline. Evan powered up the hill, knowing that perhaps he would have a chance in the triathlon, not because he was stronger or faster, but because, indeed, his heart was pure.

Thirty-Five

Ancient Delphi, Greece
The night before the race

The ancient ruins of Delphi had an almost magical appeal. Evan would have found himself romanced by the setting, or the cuisine or the good-natured Greeks, but it was all spoiled as he watched McKnight prance around in front of the cameras like a white knight. McKnight led a frenzied group of media people and athletes down the main hallway of his 'vacation home' in Central Greece. "In Ancient Greece," he said, a camera trained on his face, "Delphi was regarded as the center of the earth. According to mythology, Zeus released two eagles at the opposite ends of the world and they met here in Ancient Delphi."

Evan followed at the back of the group, feeling awkward to be wearing a tuxedo after a year of squeezing into wetsuits and spandex shorts. Through the open windows, Evan heard rippling water from brooks feeding into a gorgeous alpine meadow. In the distance, he saw the Gulf of Corinth, and beyond that the majestic Evritania Mountain range.

The IOC had agreed to perform a formal reading of the Olympic Oath in McKnight's house. The enormous house was built on the side of the rugged Mount Parnassos overlooking Ancient Delphi, an archeological site in the town of Delphi, over one hundred miles northwest of Athens.

"In the 6th and 4th century," McKnight said, fixing his cherry-colored bow-tie, "Delphi drew pilgrims in search of prophecies from the oracle. The oracle's decisions influenced political and intellectual life, which included going to war as well as who would lead."

Evan supposed one could accomplish just about anything with McKnight's wealth, but he didn't think that included building a house in a World Heritage site. Evan didn't want to think about who McKnight would have had to bribe to achieve it.

McKnight gave the cameras a dazzling smile and then glanced over at David Thompson. "If you will all please follow me to the courtyard, Mr. Thompson will lead the *Aletheian* athletes in the reading of the Olympic oath." David didn't look happy to be there, but followed McKnight like everyone else, Olympic Charter in hand.

The registered athletes mostly kept to themselves. Most prominent in the lineup was Julius Leventis, a physiological wonder. Leaning against a wall confidently was the Tanzanian ultra-distance runner and multiple winner of the *Ironman* triathlon. It was rumored that the 55-year-old was a Masaai warrior before becoming a distance runner. Beside him, with his arms folded across his chest, was a barrel-chest and burly Danish man who had been a professional power lifter before a career-ending shoulder injury led him to endurance sports. Toward the middle of the group, looking meek, but aware and calculating, was Dan Gardner, a psychology professor who ran ultras as a hobby. There were only three women in the race, one of whom was 27-year-old Isabella Dawson.

As the group walked down the long hallway, McKnight pointed to notable pieces of Greek statues, pottery, and paintings he had collected. He nodded at an ancient Greek pot with detailed drawings of figures as silhouettes. "In Ancient Greece, pots like these were worthless." He chuckled. "Now they're worth millions."

McKnight gave Evan a subtle grin. "Ancient potters were famous for their competitiveness." He looked at Julius, a potter by trade. "Perhaps our local potter could say more."

Julius didn't seem amused, but obliged. "Yes, they were constantly trying to outdo each other in their designs."

McKnight wrapped his hands around a pot's orange-red surface. "I bought this wine jar from The British Museum for $3.4 million. It was made in Athens around 540 BC." The side of the jar showed a silhouetted man towering over a female warrior on her knees. The women's hand held a spear, though not in an attack position. "This jar depicts Achilles slaying Penthesilea, an Amazonian queen in Greek mythology."

"It's a great story." Julius pulled back his broad shoulders. "At the end of the *Iliad*, Homer writes about the Trojans' defeat. After Achilles killed Hector, he returned his corpse back to the King of Troy." A cameraman moved in for a close-up of Julius. "As the Trojans grieved the loss of Hector, Penthesilea and her female warriors launched a devastating attack on the Greeks." Julius took the wine jar from McKnight. "On this jar, Penthesilea comes face-to-face with Achilles."

Evan watched McKnight as he played with the bracelet of Achilles he had stolen from Lucian. Evan wanted to rip it off his hand, but managed to stop himself.

Julius continued. "The jar shows Achilles thrusting his spear into Penthesilea. You can see that she didn't use her spear to fight back. It is said that her pose is "ambiguous"—half fleeing, half fighting." The camera came in closer. "Just as Achilles landed his final blow, he met eyes with Penthesilea, and many say that at this moment—"

"*They fell in love.*" Evan turned to see Dana. Her black hair was shortened to shoulder-length, and she was wearing a black gown with a dark-red scarf. Evan thought she looked more enchanting than ever.

McKnight laughed, and welcomed Dana into his arms. "There you are! Everyone, I'd like to introduce Dana Brines... my fiancée."

Evan's mouth fell open. He was flabbergasted. *Fiancée?*

Dana didn't look happy at the announcement. "Honey, I thought we were going to wait to tell people?"

"Nonsense! I want to shout it from the top of Mount Olympus!" McKnight looked into the camera, adopting a boastful tone. "If everything goes to plan, I'll be shouting it from the top of Egaleo Mountain in first place." He scanned the athletes with a grin on his face. Some chuckled, most looked indifferent. Isabella shook her head, unimpressed.

"Oh, I'm just joking," McKnight said. "Anyway, you may recognize Dana as the head of DARPA. Since the *Excelsior* program has been discontinued, it no longer needs funding, and we can finally 'go public' with our relationship." Dana squeezed in close to McKnight, wrapped her arm around him and squeezed his wrist. She shot the camera a grin. "Not *too* public, dear."

Everyone laughed at that, except for Evan.

Thirty-Six

The thought of marrying McKnight had been unappealing when Dana was in her twenties, but now it was as attractive as a bad car accident. Sure, the billionaire was sexy, powerful, and had a terrific body, but he was a natural-born liar, a bullshit artist, and she loathed his deceptive nature. Still, she maintained her pretense. She needed him to believe that she loved him, whatever that took.

She felt McKnight's hand graze the small of her back as she stepped down a cobblestone path, an ancient trail known as *The Sacred Way*. The last one out of the house. McKnight addressed the group. "If you all will follow me along *The Sacred Way*, we'll read the Olympic Oath at the Temple of Apollo."

The group entered Ancient Delphi through the main entrance. McKnight had "rented" the archeological site for the evening. The sun was setting, and Dana watched as several tour buses loaded visitors to leave for the night.

McKnight's head was high. "In Ancient Greece, *The Sacred Way* was lined with statues and treasures—gifts from Greek city states. The gifts commemorated victories; others were powerful demonstrations of a state's wealth and might."

"Can you feel the special power of this place?" McKnight asked with wonder in his voice. "If you listen closely, you might hear the footsteps of ancient pilgrims."

The footsteps of ancient pilgrims? Good Lord. Dana forced a smile. He really was in love with the sound of his own voice.

McKnight led the group past crumbling artifacts. "This pedestal used to hold the statue of a bull, a gift from the city of Corfu."

Dana had been finding it increasingly difficult to tolerate McKnight, despite the necessity of it. Every day his ego grew larger, his delusions of grandeur stronger. The training had inflated his own image of himself, exacerbated in large part by the Nan Airs' power, most likely. He'd been a megalomaniac *before* the world ever knew about *The Aletheia*, but now he was a monster, a man obsessed with his own myth. Dana thought it was amusing that the race would end on Egaleo Mountain where the tyrant Xerxes once had a throne. McKnight, like Xerxes, thought of himself as godlike.

Masterson had done a remarkable job distributing Nan Airs. The chance to finally scare people away from doping had been enough to motivate him, even before Dana's money. He reported that nearly three quarters of the athletes at the upcoming Olympics would likely supplement. She still couldn't believe how they had clamored for her Nan Airs, eager to compete under the potent effects of DARPA's elixir. She thought of her Davos speech, made for the sake of spreading the word. People were going to get their enhanced Olympics, after all.

Dana tried to tune out McKnight's voice, and she fiddled with a small device in her pocket. The triggering mechanism would, if she so pleased, disintegrate the Nan Airs in McKnight's blood, causing a fatal systemic reaction. She had switched McKnight's Nan Airs with the lethal version weeks ago. One touch of the button, and it could be the shortest engagement in history. It was tempting to end his life right there. To make him pay in front of the cameras. But she would wait. The irony—and beauty—was that she wouldn't have to bring McKnight to his knees. McKnight would do that himself. She had given him his own triggering device, telling him that Luke had been given the lethal version of the respirocytes. No doubt, he would press the button if Luke got too close during the race. Putting McKnight's death in his own hands freed her to concentrate on the Olympians.

* * *

David Thompson stood in the middle of a circle in the Temple of Apollo, at the center of the sanctuary. There was gravitas in his voice. "'Citius, Altius,

Fortius.'" He paused dramatically. "'Faster, higher, stronger.' The phrase came from Pierre de Coubertin, the founder of the International Olympic Committee in 1894."

"For over a century, this phrase has been a touchstone for champions. But running faster, jumping higher, becoming stronger takes discipline and hard work, one could say *suffering*. Over the next three to four days, you will suffer even more."

Thompson lifted the Olympic Charter, a thin booklet with the Olympic rings drawn on the cover. "The Olympic Charter says that 'the practice of sport is a human right, and that every individual can participate, without discrimination of any kind and in the Olympic spirit, which requires mutual understanding with a spirit of friendship, solidarity, and fair play.'"

Thompson paused. "Coubertin introduced another motto that I want to leave you with before the gun fires tomorrow morning. 'The most important thing,' Coubertin said, 'is not to win... but to take part.'"

"So now I am to lead you in a variation of the Olympic Oath," Thompson said. "Please repeat after me: I promise that we shall take part in these Games, respecting and abiding by the rules that govern them, in the true spirit of sportsmanship, for the glory of sport and the honor of our teams."

The racers there repeated the words. How many of them meant them though? Dana couldn't tell.

McKnight strolled into the circle's center, clapping his hands. "Fine speech, David." More clapping followed and the cameras soaked up the moment. "Thank you for those inspirational words."

Thompson couldn't really believe what he'd said, could he? Dana thought he'd lost touch with what the Olympic Games had become. 'Taking part... solidarity... *fair play?*' Coubertin's spirit was dead. The Games—modern sports, for that matter—had become a traveling circus. Reading oaths wouldn't change that. Only what Dana had planned could.

McKnight led the group on, into the ancient theater. "Plays were per-formed in this theater, which once held 5,000 spectators during the Pythian Games, an event for athletics but also music and performing arts, like plays. The *Aletheia* is similar to a play. Each participant is not unlike an actor; each of us wears a masks. Whatever mask you are wearing, the race will cast it off to reveal your true nature." He raised his hands. "Now sit, please. Think of me now as an ancient bard, a storyteller. I will finish with the story of Achilles."

Everyone sat, including Dana.

McKnight waited dramatically for his big moment. "Athletes of the Aletheia, we have taken the Olympic oath. We heard the Olympic motto. I ask you one more important question: what will your legend be? How will you be remembered? Tomorrow there will be no gods with you, no divine beings over your shoulder. Only you will be responsible for your own destiny. How will you choose?"

Thirty-Seven

Central Greece

Despite Evan's brush with heat stroke, he and Isabella had kept an incredibly fast pace on their bikes. Within the first hour of riding together, they had passed two athletes, moving them into sixth and seventh. According to Tim's scouting, there were only a few riders between them and Luke. After that, there would only be McKnight. But Isabella's support man wasn't so sure. "Forget about McKnight," he said through the window of his car. "He's too far ahead now."

Evan accelerated his pace, Isabella trying her hardest to keep up. An hour passed and the two blew past another athlete, moving into fourth and fifth. McKnight was still in first, his brother in second. Evan spotted Julius in third place, nearing a one-lane tunnel in the side of a mountain. Isabella looked tired, but seemed to find energy as Evan shot off to pursue Julius. Evan made up the ground on Julius, came up behind him, and executed a slingshot around him.

Julius looked floored, but said nothing as Evan zipped around him. The tunnel was maybe fifty feet away when a figure caught his eye, a man above the road. He looked like—

Pieces of dirt and tiny pebbles rained down, and then the street filled with stones the size of baseballs. By the time Evan and Julius realized it was a landslide, there was nowhere to go. A rock struck Evan in the shoulder.

"Go back!" Evan yelled to Isabella, but she was holding her head, having already been hit. More rocks fell, increasing in size. Then a thick sheet of dirt and mud blanketed the three athletes, knocking them off their bikes. Evan pushed himself off the pavement, but was hit in the neck by another rock. Julius was also being pelted, his face bloody. Through the haze of debris and falling stones, Evan squinted at the figure on the ledge. His first instinct had been correct—it was McKnight who had caused this mess.

A rock struck Evan on the temple and his world became foggy. In his stupor, he became a passive observer to the carnage. He watched, in slow motion, as dirt poured off the ledge like a fountain, burying Julius and Isabella. He tasted dirt. Sounds fell away, but Evan still saw McKnight duck behind a tree. He reappeared, pushing a massive boulder with his shoulder. In a panic, Evan crawled on his belly toward Isabella. She crawled to him, too. Julius looked on, his body badly bruised from the falling rocks. Was he really going to die like this—crushed by a boulder on some no-name road in Greece? The road continued to clutter with dirt and rocks, but the biggest rock had yet to come. About ten feet from Isabella, Evan reached out a hand.

Thirty-Eight

Central Greece

The boulder was McKnight's height, and a bitch to move. He found he could barely budge it with his shoulder, so he grabbed a thick tree branch to use as leverage. Slowly, he edged the big rock into position, directly in Evan's path. He saw Evan pathetically reach his hand toward the Spanish girl. To think, a few minutes prior he had considered Evan a legitimate threat in *The Aletheia*. Perhaps he should just let Evan lie there and suffer? Was the boulder overkill? No, he had learned with Masterson that there was something empowering about extinguishing a life.

McKnight took a deep breath and slammed his shoulder into it, enough to get it rolling, a few inches at first, then more. After a couple of feet, it was a run-away train on a perfect trajectory toward Evan.

* * *

Evan knew he was dead. Watching the boulder pick up steam, he squeezed Isabella's hand as she lowered her head. Evan flipped onto his back and looked up to the sky. It turned out that he wasn't the hero after all. Competing with cutthroats like McKnight was a losing battle. But Evan was glad that his brother was in first place now. Most importantly, Evan was proud of himself, and that he had reclaimed some self-respect by admitting that he had taken the shortcut. He watched the boulder skip off the tip of the ledge and plummet to the ground like a missile—

Out of nowhere, Julius stepped in front of Evan and threw his back into the boulder, crumpling his body under the weight. The big man let out a horrifying grunt as the boulder smashed into him. The movement wasn't enough to stop it, but the impact with the massive form of Julius was enough to knock it from its path. It rolled past Evan to slam into the tunnel wall.

Evan scurried across the road toward Julius on his hands and knees. He could barely bring himself to look at what lay there. The man was broken. His chest was caved in, his face shattered. Julius breathed heavily, and there was a loud wheeze with each breath. He tried to speak.

"Evan..." He spit a gob of blood onto his chin and cringed as a wave of pain washed over him.

"Julius, why did you do that? Why?"

Julius blinked slowly and then held his gaze on a passing cloud. "Because I am no longer ashamed of what I did. This... I hope it is enough. I am proud now." His breathing slowed, his eyes looking heavy. His chest stayed in place and the life drifted from his eyes. It seemed like a heavy price for redemption, but it was one Evan could at least begin to understand.

* * *

McKnight couldn't believe what he had seen. Angrily, he stirred up more loose rocks to start a bigger landslide, one that would do the job. He smiled as a river of rocks and dirt tumbled toward the road. He scrambled down the backside of the hill to his bike. He would catch up to Luke and inform him that his brother was dead. If he couldn't beat Luke, he'd trigger his Nan Airs, and two Galloways would be dead.

* * *

Tim parked his car on the side of the road, and Evan watched his friend grab his cell phone, likely to report the accident. As he extended the antenna, Evan was struck by an idea that perhaps Dana's triggering device emitted a high-energy radio frequency. At a high enough frequency, an electromagnetic pulse that harmonized with the Nan Airs would no doubt destroy them. And if the nano-sized machines were broken up in the bloodstream, they would cause a systemic immune reaction, which would be lethal.

Evan heard a tremendous roar overhead, and knew another avalanche was coming. Evan sprinted to his bike.

"Tim! Dana's device: I think it emits a high-energy EMP. Figure out a way to interfere with the signal. I'll meet you at the opening ceremony."

Evan mounted his bike as dirt crashed around him. Evan sped into the tunnel as larger rocks rained down. He looked back and saw the face of the mountain fall into the road, closing off the entrance to the tunnel. With no passage for Tim or Isabella, Evan was on his own in pursuit of Luke and McKnight.

Thirty-Nine

Evan felt a sense of elation as race volunteers waved him through grid-like streets of Sparta and into the second transition area to finish the 700-mile cycling portion. *The Aletheia* was far from over, however. He still had to run 131 miles. Two days on a bicycle had wreaked havoc on his body. The skin on his ass felt like hamburger. The riding position had also put pressure on his hands and neck and, at times, his neck gave out from fatigue. Some athletes had actually applied duct tape from the back of their heads to their belts to keep their necks upright.

Evan arrived at transition and jumped off his bike. The original plan had been to sleep for a few hours in transition, but he couldn't afford the loss of time. He didn't see either of them, which meant they had already left for the finish line on Eglaeo Mountain. Evan rustled through a duffle bag Tim had left for him.

Evan wasted no time in transition. He stowed his bike and then quickly laced up his running shoes. He picked through pre-packaged meals in plastic containers, mostly chicken breasts, eggs, bread, and copious amounts of vegetables and fruits. He took four ibuprofens and washed it down with a Gu packet. It was time to run.

* * *

It was midnight and the air was a chilly 35 degrees. Evan's headlamp illuminated a small patch of road in front of him, but everything else was pitch-black. He passed through a poorly lit village, and wrestled on a fleece jacket. He passed through another town, running on a paved road. It was all blurring together now. The road changed to dirt, climbed through the hills, and then dipped back into a plateau.

The first challenge on the running portion of the race was a short hill climb up Mount Tegea, just outside the city of Tripolis. Evan took a deep breath at the base of the hill, lowered his head, and charged upward. Halfway up, he felt like a zombie. He had used up so much energy trying to make up time after the landslide that he was dangerously close to complete exhaustion. Somehow, he reached the summit. It was a mini victory. He would need many more. This run was about survival now. At this point, he was just trying not to fall asleep standing up.

Perhaps it was the force of running downhill, but Evan began to feel a dull ache in his left knee. The arch of his foot hurt as well, a nagging injury from his training with Lucian. The ibuprofen barely put a dent in the discomfort, so he grabbed a couple of painkillers from the bag around his waist and swallowed them with water.

As Evan approached the next challenge, Mount Sangas, which rose 3,940 feet, his run had deteriorated into an awkward shuffle that was half-jog, half-walk. At the base of the mountain, Evan entered a narrow pathway that was rocky and difficult to navigate. He felt utterly spent. He didn't know how far ahead Luke and McKnight were. Ten minutes into the hill climb, Evan tripped and fell hard. He rose slowly, clutching a bloodied elbow.

Evan had reached his wits end. The revolt he knew his body would inevitably stage finally came. Partly, it was a lack of sleep. He craved sleep at all times and had nearly nodded off while running numerous times. He began to see shadows flit across the road, like mountain ghosts. The rocks leapt out at him, as if defending their hill side. In his studies as a limit physiologist, Evan had heard about athletes reporting hallucinations during ultra-endurance events. Severe sleep deprivation caused them to literally experience nightmares while awake.

Evan dropped his head between his knees. His legs felt wobbly, as if they might give out at any moment. He tried to start running again, but his legs betrayed him and he toppled over. His face hit the ground and his arms fell behind him helplessly. This feeling was quite different from "hitting the wall." It was even different to nearly drowning a couple of days ago, different to heat stroke, or to the pain he'd felt being pelted by falling rocks during the landslide. This was a total body shut down. He buried his face in the dirt, closed his eyes, and knew the race was over. And then he heard it...

"Get up," a voice whispered, as if it were a foot away from Evan's ear.

Evan didn't voice a response... he thought it: "*I can't.*"

Out of the darkness, a ghostly figure appeared. Evan knew it wasn't real; clearly it was a hallucination. But the apparition was unmistakable: *It was Lucian.*

The presence floated toward Evan. The voice was soft. "Get up, Evan."

Evan knew he was delirious, but he couldn't stop the tears from welling up in his eyes. "I don't need your help."

"Maybe not. But the world still needs its symbol."

"I'm not good enough," Evan insisted.

"Who said that you had to be?"

Perhaps that was the truth Evan had been trying to get a grip on. Truly, everyone seemed to be trying to do the best they could. And yet so often they screwed up, even when they were trying to do the "right" thing. But if everyone made mistakes, then maybe succeeding wasn't the most important thing.

"You have made mistakes, Evan. And you will make more. All we can do is move on, and remind ourselves that we will always be tested, and sometimes we will fail to live up to our highest ideals."

It was true. Perfect integrity wasn't possible. People were, as Lucian said, imperfect by nature. They were always seemingly in conflict with themselves, subject to a spectrum of competing feelings. A realistic and humanistic story of life accounted for the successes *and* the accidents, the triumphs *and* the failures, the progresses *and* the steps back.

"Get up," Lucian said in a stern voice. "Failing is one thing. Giving up is another. Your brother needs you."

Tears streamed down Evan's face. Somehow though, he forced himself to his feet. He didn't dare to think about winning now, but maybe he could make it to the finish, perhaps a few hours away.

* * *

Evan looked down the flat road, and guessed Egaleo Mountain was maybe ten miles away. While the peak was only 1,539 feet high, and not as awe-inspiring as Mount Olympus, it still felt like a daunting prospect. But also a relief. The finish line was close now. So very close.

In the distance, he saw two runners side-by-side. Evan took off in a full sprint.

Evan had always had a deep curiosity about the human body. It was what had drawn him to physiology, the study of how the body functions. It was remarkable to him that just a few hours before he had been paralyzed with exhaustion. Now, he was running at full speed, psychologically prepared to run the final miles faster than he had run the first few.

In exercise physiology, there was a theory known as the Central Governor Theory, which suggested that there is a circuit in the brain that "governs" the body's energy supply. When this pathway of brain cells thinks the body's energy stores are low, it uses pain signals to urge the person to stop and rest. However, the central governor is overly conservative, and signals the body to stop long before supplies are fully depleted. Despite the fact that Evan was in immense pain, he still had an untapped reservoir of energy. He pushed harder, knowing that his brain was underestimating him, making a conservative estimate of his energy… his potential.

As he gained ground on McKnight and Luke, he thought about McKnight's comment on CNBC. "There are no limits," he had said. Lucian had said the same thing. They were right, Evan thought. The ego had limits, but the body, one's "true self" was indeed without limits. Unlike McKnight and Luke, Evan hadn't needed a drug or a technology to go past his.

Forty

The moon had dipped below the horizon, and the sky was filled with clouds. The rain began abruptly. Evan could barely see as he sprinted through the sheets of rain up the dirt pathway on Egaleo Mountain. Though his visibility was impaired, he was sure he was on Luke's heels, and that McKnight was just ahead of him.

Luke looked back and saw his brother. "What the—"

As Evan came up alongside him, Luke increased his speed up the steep path, gaining a few feet. Evan pushed hard, passing Luke. The back and forth continued until they approached McKnight.

"Evan!" Luke screamed into the wind. "*How are you doing this?*"

Evan ignored that. Every muscle in Evan's body was crying out in pain.

Hearing Luke's voice, McKnight craned his head back. He probably didn't expect Evan to be behind him. Evan watched him pull a black device from his pocket. Was that the same device Tim had showed him on the first day of the race? McKnight pressed a button. Just then, Luke dropped to the ground, holding a hand to his chest.

Evan knelt beside his brother who looked disoriented and in severe pain. "Are you okay?"

Luke growled. "Damn, that stings."

Evan knew the device was Dana's. If he'd understood what it did correctly, then it had disintegrated the Nan Airs in Luke's bloodstream. Soon, his immune system would attack every system in his body. Through the rain, Evan was surprised to see McKnight doubled over, too. Clearly, McKnight had betrayed Luke by giving him the lethal version of the Nan Airs, but why was McKnight doubled over? Had someone given *him* the lethal version? It didn't take long to figure out how it must have happened: Dana had switched his healthy Nan Airs with the lethal version.

Evan tried to lift Luke, but his brother smacked his hand away.

"Get the hell out of here!" Luke said, cringing from the pain. He pointed at the finish line, now only half a mile away. "There's the finish." His tone was self-loathing. "Congratulations, you're going to win. You still have a perfect record. You've beaten me in everything we've ever done together."

McKnight was fifty feet ahead, still crouched in agony. To the side of the road was the historical site of King Xerxe's throne, overlooking the city of Athens.

"*Come on,*" Evan said with urgency. "We're so close to the end."

Luke swung at Evan, and the punch connected. Evan recoiled and held his jaw in agony. For some reason, he remembered the meaning of "Aletheia," that was "being unconcealed," or "in a state of not being hidden." What had the race revealed about Evan? Suddenly, he took off at full speed toward the finish line.

As Evan passed him, McKnight burst from his crouched position, smashed into Evan, and tackled him.

The burst of effort took Evan completely by surprise. It carried him off the pathway before Evan could stop it, heading for the edge of the cliff. Evan felt like he was riding the wing of an F-16 on McKnight's shoulder. Then the two of them slammed into the ground, just feet from the edge. They landed awkwardly, with Evan on top. From where he was, he could see the space beyond, hundreds of feet down.

He brought his fist down on McKnight's head, but McKnight was unfazed. Then Evan grabbed McKnight's face and pressed his finger into the center of his eye patch. McKnight howled in pain and heaved Evan toward the lip of the cliff. He dragged his hands across the loose dirt as his body slipped over the edge. His fingers gripped a small rock, as McKnight lumbered over, still in agony from the activated Nan Airs.

"You really thought I was going to let you just jog by me and win?"

McKnight was then rocked from behind, as Luke tackled him to the ground. Evan pulled himself to safety and tried to find an entry point as Luke and McKnight wrestled. Luke mounted McKnight and punched him in the face repeatedly. McKnight powered up, flipping him over his head. Both scrambled back to their feet.

The three stood there, staring at each other, breathing heavily. The rain lashed into them, the wind howling around them as it swept across the mountain.

Luke pointed at McKnight. He was unsteady on his feet now. "You gave me the lethal Nan Airs? I thought you were my friend!"

"Please, I used you." McKnight coughed blood into his hand, and laughed to himself. "Apparently Dana used me."

Luke looked pale now. "How do we reverse it?"

Evan shook his head. There was no obvious way to clear the bloodstream of the detonated Nan Airs.

"There's no cure," McKnight said, wiping rain from his face. "We paid Weng to create a deadly version. He didn't find an antidote."

Evan glared at McKnight. "Which you used to kill your own son."

McKnight's face turned sour. "My son was a necessary test subject. And he'd already shamed our family's name by getting caught doping."

"The apple doesn't fall far from the tree," Luke said.

"What does it matter anymore?" McKnight shook his head. "I guess she got me back."

But what if it wasn't just McKnight? Evan thought back to the conversation he'd had with Dana on the plane. No, she couldn't be...

"How many athletes will have used Nan Airs for the Olympics?" Evan asked.

McKnight shrugged. "Like I care."

"Probably any that can get their hands on them," Luke said. He winced at another spasm of pain.

Which might be hundreds, if Evan was right. "If she lied to you about this, then what if she gave the others lethal respirocytes too? She's out of her mind." Evan shook his head. "McKnight, you need to talk her out of it!"

"She won't listen to me, or you." He lifted the triggering device. "She's the one who gave me this, after all. I said Luke might be able to beat me. She knew I'd use it eventually and that, when I did, it would kill me." He shook his head. "If it wasn't for you and your goddamn will to win, I wouldn't have *had* to use it. And I wouldn't be a dead man right now."

McKnight was wounded, but he took off toward the finish line. He didn't get five feet before Evan tackled him to the ground. McKnight was back on his feet until Luke punched him in the jaw, which sent McKnight skipping backwards and over the ledge. Evan and Luke scurried to the edge, and a hand reached out.

"You're already dead," McKnight said, gripping Luke's neck. "What's the difference if it's now or twenty minutes from now?"

But Luke was defiant, and cocked his fist back. "This is for getting me hooked on drugs again." He smashed his fist into McKnight's face, freeing his grip.

McKnight was loose for a moment, floating, until Evan snatched his wrist.

Luke looked at Evan in disbelief. "What are you doing?"

"We can't let him die."

Luke's voice was soft. "Drop him, Evan." Luke shook Evan's hands to try and break the bond. "Do it!" he screamed. Evan held tight, but the rain was loosening his grip.

Evan had something to say. "You wanted to win the *Aletheia* and then parade into Athens like some hero."

McKnight's hand slipped an inch. Evan looked back at the Xerxe's throne. "You're no different than the tyrant who sat there." He slipped further. "You'll die here today." Evan stared into McKnight's eyes. "And your name will die with you."

McKnight snarled, and then opened his hand, releasing himself. He obviously didn't want Evan to choose the moment of his death. Evan didn't break eye contact as McKnight plummeted into the darkness below.

In the palm of Evan's hand was Lucian's bracelet of Achilles.

Forty-One

Evan could barely hold Luke upright as the two hobbled toward the finish line, a few hundred feet away. Luke kept falling to the ground, his breathing labored. The rain had stopped, but the road was still damp, and several hundred people huddled around the strip of tape at the finish line, and cheering and shouting in the bleachers as Evan and Luke approached.

Luke rested his head between his knees. "I can't make it." He tipped over and heaved. "Just go."

Evan thought about the Aletheia's premise. McKnight's voice at Delphi still rung in his ears: a race that revealed *who you were*. As he thought about the runners closing in somewhere behind them, Evan thought about making a mad dash for the finish line, and leaving his brother there. Wasn't it better that at least one of them finished first? He'd be the victor, finally get his chance to shine, and to show that "good guys" could get the best of them all; it would be a defiant middle finger to the cheaters of the human race. His brother's words were clear. *Just go*. He slid his hands into his brother's. "I'm sorry, Luke, but one of us needs to win this."

Luke was weak, but he nodded, looking proud for Evan. "You earned it, man."

"I'll come back after with help." Evan sprinted away and chewed up space between him and the finish line. What a feeling it would be when he crossed. What a statement. So close now. Twenty feet. Ten feet. The crowd was in pandemonium. Three feet and it would all be over. But with only two steps to go, Evan stopped. The spectators became silent, stunned.

Evan turned and saw Luke. His brother was coughing violently, but managed to rise, his knees quivering. *What am I doing?* Evan thought. Not a half hour ago Evan was conversing with a hallucination of Lucian. Promising to look out for his brother. Now? His relationship with Luke wasn't perfect. All the bickering, the conflict, and competition. It didn't matter, because they were family and he loved him.

He didn't need the race to prove that. He hadn't won the race yet, but he had, indeed, changed just as Lucian had said he would need to over the course of training. He was no longer that weakling that Dana had taken advantage of; no longer vulnerable to the wicked and the corrupt. The race had sculpted him, had stripped away all the excess to reveal strength, power, goodness… virtue. Evan ran toward his brother. This wasn't Evan's race to win. It was *their* race to win.

Evan yanked Luke up by the back of his pants. "We're finishing together."

Luke was sick, but he could barely hold back the emotion. "Am I going to die, Evan?"

"My friend Tim might be able to help. Let's win this thing first." Evan knew there wasn't an antidote, but maybe he could think of something. He turned and saw two runners closing in on them. They needed to hurry. Luke collapsed to the ground again, holding his chest as he wheezed loudly. "Dana's right about one thing. People like me deserve to die, Ev." He let out a deep, guttural cough.

"Don't say that."

"Anything I ever won, I scammed my way into it."

Evan looked around. He could see runners behind them now. They'd built up a lead, but they'd spent it fighting McKnight and hobbling towards the finish. The runners were almost on top of them. The crowd hushed.

"You listen to me carefully," Evan said, "because this is important. We need to let ourselves off the hook. For the mistakes we've made. I don't care what you did. I don't care what I did. We need to forgive ourselves."

Luke coughed violently and then lifted his head slowly to meet Evan's eyes. His brother looked more innocent in that moment, a far cry from the impulsive junkie who had let drugs get the best of him. The sun was beginning to rise now, casting sharp rays of light across the Athenian countryside. Evan put his hands underneath Luke's armpits and dragged him, as he sat looking out toward Athens, his feet making lines in the dirt.

They were twenty feet away from the finish. Luke coughed and looked up with smiling eyes. "I'm sorry, man. For everything. I love you." Somehow, he managed to stand, wobbling left and right.

Evan had never heard that from Luke. "I love you, Luke." Evan smiled proudly. "Now let's go win this thing."

Evan wrapped an arm around Luke's waist and the two broke into a clumsy jog. Spectators went crazy as they lumbered down the last stretch of road. Evan saw the time clock over the finish line, which read: 3 days, 10 hours, and 21 minutes. At the same time, Evan and Luke broke through the tape. And, suddenly it was over. Just like that.

Over a loudspeaker, a man announced Evan and Luke's names as the winners of the *Aletheia*. "Ladies and gentleman," he yelled, "It appears we have a tie for the win between two brothers from the States. Let's hear it for *Evan and Luke Galloway!*"

Media people, spectators, race volunteers, and medical professionals rushed forwards. Evan ducked his head as a volunteer put a medal around his neck, but tried to push past them.

Tim emerged from the crowd, sweeping Evan up in a hearty bear hug. "You won!"

"No time for celebration," Evan said, setting Luke down.

Luke hacked up a dark-red ball of spit. "What's wrong with him?"

Evan rushed to Luke's side. "Nan Airs, the lethal version. McKnight detonated them with one of Dana's devices."

"Oh, no," Tim said. "Where's McKnight?"

"He's dead." Evan raised his voice over the cheering. "Can we clear the respirocytes from his system, Tim?"

Tim paused. "We simulated every contingency imaginable," he said.

"There are a thousand ways the Nan Airs could malfunction: Jammed rotor banks, glucose power plants shutting down, plugged exhaust ports—everything *except* complete structural failure."

"But it's happened," Evan said.

Luke coughed up blood. "Just do something."

Tim started to talk, thinking aloud. "The injection probably delivered around 20 to 30 million respirocytes into your bloodstream before they detonated. Each broke into a few thousand fragments. Your bloodstream is so saturated that the fragments have bubbled up into your mouth."

Evan racked his brains for a solution. How could blood be cleared of the Nan Airs, he thought. As he pondered, he mindlessly spun Lucian's bracelet on his wrist. Then an idea struck him. He removed the bracelet and knelt down, bringing the bracelet slowly toward Luke's saliva.

Tim asked, "What are you—?"

The group watched as a mist rose off the ground and stuck to the bracelet.

"Yes, of course," Tim said. His eyes were wide as he got the idea. "*Brilliant.* A magnet could pull the fragments from his body." He rubbed his chin. "But, it would need to be quite strong—"

Evan was already ahead of him. He shouted to an emergency medical technician. "Hey!"

Luke was sweating profusely. He was also much paler than before. He coughed up more sputum and blood.

The EMT jogged over. Evan asked, "Do you guys have an MRI?"

The EMT laughed. "On the top of Egaleo Mountain? No, sorry, forgot to put one in my backpack."

"Well, where then?" Evan asked, annoyed.

"There's one in the medical facility at the Olympic stadium in Athens. Aren't you guys supposed to be there for the end of the Opening Ceremony?"

Evan lifted his brother off the ground, and looked at the EMT. "We need to get there as fast as possible."

"Your ride's right over there." The EMT pointed to a chariot attached to two horses with a man ready to drive. "Or we have an ambulance."

Evan wanted to shake his head, but it *was* going to the stadium. "Thanks. My brother… we need to get him to an MRI as fast as possible."

"The medical facility at the stadium is probably the closest," the EMT said. "They like to be able to scan injuries on site."

Tim grabbed Evan's shoulder. "An MRI might work, but it's going to hurt like hell, you know?"

"Worse than a 700-mile triathlon?"

"Good point."

Evan helped Luke stumble into the chariot. When Luke was settled in the back, he looked at Tim and Weng. "Once I get him to the MRI, I'm going after Dana, but I need you two to figure out a way of blocking the signal from her triggering device, just in case I can't get to her in time."

Tim looked over at Evan. "You said the triggering device works by emitting an electromagnetic pulse that harmonizes with the Nan Airs, right?"

"That's what I think," Evan said. "We need something that will interfere with the EMP."

Tim looked thoughtful. "We could try a faraday cage."

Evan nodded. "Yes, that might work."

Luke coughed up more blood. "What the hell is a faraday cage?"

Tim explained it. "An electromagnetic pulse is a burst of radiant energy, emitted during a solar flare or a nuclear blast. An EMP typically destroys any electronic equipment in the pulse radius. A faraday cage blocks an electromagnetic signal. A cell phone, for example, would be protected in one during an electromagnetic disturbance."

Evan tried to think. They would need to make one, but that would be simple enough. Any surrounding metal structure might work, the metal causing the signal to flow around the surface, not through it.

An idea struck him. "What about the thermal blankets that marathon runners use to keep warm at the end of a race?"

Tim nodded. "That might work, if it isn't open."

Evan needed to make sure. "So this material would block the signal from Dana's triggering device?"

"With enough of it, yeah, I think it might."

That was as good as they were going to get. Evan looked around. "I'll make sure Dana doesn't press the button to activate the Nan Airs. You two try and find as many of these thermal blankets as you can."

Tim handed Evan a cell phone. "I'll be in touch."

Part III

*"We claim to be just and upright. No wrath from us will
come stealthily to the one who holds out clean hands, and
he will go through life unharmed. But whoever sins and
hides his blood-stained hands, as avengers of bloodshed we appear
against him to the end, presenting ourselves as upright witnesses for the dead."*

– THE ERINYES. AESCHYLUS, EUMENIDES 310

Forty-Two

Athens, Greece

The last time Dana had held a gun she was fifteen years old. Her father had taken her to a shooting range. She had learned quickly. Load, safety off, point-and-shoot, more or less. She had stolen the Beretta in her jacket pocket from McKnight. She didn't necessarily intend to use it, but better to have it and not need it than to need it and not have it. She learned that from her dad, too. Getting it into the stadium hadn't been easy, but she'd managed to use her position to get in without being searched.

She glanced at the map of the Spiros Louis Olympic stadium in her hand, and took a left down a narrow hall. She heard the roar of the spectators in the stands, as they watched the opening ceremony unfold. The artistic program was a spectacle of dancing, marching, and gymnastics wrapped around the grandiose theme of Ancient Greece's Olympic past.

She strode through a set of double doors, and arrived at the room she wanted. *Main Operations Center*. Filled with producers, journalists, and editors, it was the so-called "heart" of the Games' communications and broadcasting. David Thompson would be there.

After Dana activated the Nan Airs within the stadium, athletes who supplemented would drop like flies. At that point, the broadcast would cut away. No producer in their right mind would broadcast the brutal death of almost 10,000 people, let alone beloved Olympic athletes. Dana needed the cameras to keep rolling. They had to broadcast the carnage. People needed to see what happened to cheaters or it wouldn't stop the next wave of them. It wouldn't shock them into stopping. Reaching the operations center, she leaned against the wall and clicked off the gun's safety. Then she turned and booted the doors open.

Forty-Three

6 miles from Athens center

A cheery, overweight man leapt from the front seat of the chariot. "All aboard. My name's Theodore."

Evan propped Luke up in the backseat. "I'm Evan," he said. "This is my brother Luke."

"Yes, I know." Theodore hopped into the front seat and grabbed the reins to the horses. "Transporting the winners of *the Aletheia* is a tremendous honor."

Luke let out a series of severe coughs. Theodore examined Luke closely. "What's wrong with him?" His eyes narrowed. "Hey, he's not going to barf in my chariot, is he?"

Evan was quick to respond. "Just get us to Athens as fast as possible."

Luke didn't have much time left when he could barely hold himself upright in the backseat.

"You got it," Theodore said, cracking the horse's reins. "Athens is six miles from here." As the chariot lurched forward, Theodore continued. "The ceremony's artistic program is likely finishing now. We should arrive near the end of the athletes' procession."

"Hurry!" Evan insisted. If there had been another vehicle there, another way down… but there hadn't been. He just had to hope the chariot would be fast enough.

Evan rubbed Luke's damp hair with his head in his lap. Theodore carefully steered the chariot down the narrow paths on Egaleo Mountain. There were a couple of perilous moments, but they reached the bottom safely. At the bottom, they passed the Daphnia Monastery, which Theodore explained was an 11th century Byzantine monastery. Evan was in no mood for "fun facts," but Theodore seemed to think of himself as a tour guide, so Evan let him ramble. Just so long as he didn't slow down.

Theodore lifted his hand toward the acropolis in the Athens' center, which consisted of temple complexes, monuments, sculptures, and altars. "Athens was named after Athena, the goddess of wisdom." He explained the significance of a large structure surrounded by pillars. "That's the Parthenon. Pericles had it built as a temple dedicated to Athena."

The chariot passed the acropolis. Theodore seemed to sense Evan's curiosity. "Pericles built the Parthenon to awake a new sense of self-awareness in the people of Athens. He wanted it to be a source of inspiration, not only for the citizens of Athens, but for all of Europe, even the rest of the world."

Lucian had wanted Evan to do the same; to bring honor back to sports. Perhaps in some perverse way, Dana wanted the same thing. The way she wanted to do it, however, was enough to turn Evan's stomach.

Theodore continued to explain Pericles' vision. "Pericles had a single message with the Acropolis." He lifted his chin. "He wanted his people to remember the glorious origins of Athens. He wanted them to remember their heroic past, the great courage they had always showed in battle, especially in athletics. In some ways, Pericles thought that this had been forgotten, and the Acropolis stands here as a touchstone. After Pericles died, Athens' golden age was over." Another crack at the reins. "We're probably overdue for another."

Up ahead, looming large was the Spiros Olympic Stadium, ablaze with activity.

* * *

Dana had tied David Thompson to a chair and the fifteen or so staffers were locked in a storage room. David stared at Dana blankly, looking unnerved by Dana's irrational behavior, though far from intimidated.

"What are you trying to prove?" he said, moving his eyes up and down Dana as if she were a child. "Whatever it is, this is the wrong way to do it."

"You'll see," she said, watching the procession on the TV monitors. "I'm just waiting for our torchbearer." Dana was standing behind the communication team's executive producer as well as a technician, two men who could control the broadcast of the Olympics. They had been compliant so far, but very twitchy, wincing every time Dana swung her pistol in their direction.

"How many people will watch this?" she asked. Dana knew the broadcast of the opening ceremony would draw an enormous audience.

The producer answered her. "A billion people watched the summer Olympics in Beijing. We should top that."

"How many in the stands?"

"About 70,000."

Dana grinned. "Perfect."

"Where did Jack McKnight finish in the *Aletheia*?" The two producers looked confused.

"You don't know?"

"Know what?"

David delivered the news calmly. "He's dead."

The two men at the monitors seemed scared for their safety, wondering if the news might cause Dana to do something rash.

David was unafraid. "There was an accident, just before the finish line."

Dana tried to think. McKnight must have activated his own Nan Airs. Luke was probably closing in on him. McKnight's death raised a question though: if McKnight didn't win, who had? Perhaps, Julius? If not him, Luke?

"So, who won?" she asked.

The producer pointed to the screen. "Here they come now."

Dana watched a chariot enter the stadium. In disbelief, she saw Evan hanging out the window, looking around at the people in the stands as though searching for something. Luke was slumped in the seat next to Evan.

"No," Dana said, "that's impossible."

David had a wry smile on his face. "The brothers crossed the finish at the same time. It was a tie."

Forty-Four

Spiros Louis Olympic Stadium

Theodore steered the chariot past the main entrance and into the stadium. "And here we are, gentlemen, your big moment."

At another moment, Evan would have been in awe of the structure around him. The stadium was a true engineering marvel. Tens of thousands of spectators roared as the chariot rode onto the track, and the almost ten thousand Olympic athletes were finishing their procession around the track. Now though, he scanned the stadium, trying to work out where Dana might be.

"Who was Spiros Louis, anyway?" Evan asked, as he scanned the full stadium.

"He won the first marathon in the 1896 Olympics," Theodore answered.

Over the speakers, an anthem was blaring. Theodore yelled over the noise, "This is the Olympic anthem. Our timing is perfect, actually. This is the last part of the ceremony." He looked back at Evan proudly. "Now, we just need the final torchbearers to light the cauldron."

The stadium's roof was the structure's most striking aspect. It was a couple hundred feet off the ground, and split down the middle. Theodore saw Evan admiring it. "Marvelous, isn't it? It's called 'the jewel in the crown.'"

At the far end of the stadium was an enormous video screen, perhaps a hundred feet wide and suspended in the air. Evan's head bobbed, as the chariot lurched to a stop. Theodore leapt from his seat and opened the door. Evan lifted Luke out, but he dropped to the ground and began coughing up blood.

There was a booming voice through the stadium's speakers. "Ladies and gentleman, please welcome the two men before you, who just finished swimming, biking, and running 700 miles. Join together in celebrating the winners of the *Aletheia*: Evan and Luke Galloway!" The announcer continued. "It is now their *great* honor to carry the Olympic flame to the cauldron to officially start the Games."

"Congratulations," an athlete said dressed in a white jumpsuit, holding the Olympic torch. He handed it to Evan and lifted his chin in the cauldron's direction. "Light the flame."

Evan shook his head, pushing the torch aside. "My brother is sick," he said. "I have to get him to a medical facility. I need to get him to an MRI."

He'd only gone along with the chariot driver because he needed to be at the stadium to stop Dana. There would be a medical facility there, wouldn't there? There were too many people and athletes there for it to be any other way.

The announcer continued. "The Olympic flame commemorates Prometheus' theft of fire from the Greek God Zeus."

Evan looked left and right, searching for a medical professional. The athlete thrust the torch at him adamantly.

Evan refused. "I can't! I need to—" But Luke interrupted him.

"Evan." His voice was weak, and he looked weaker than ever.

"I'm trying to get you help—"

Luke scanned the stands slowly. "They're cheering for us."

Evan said, "I don't know how much longer you have, Luke. There's no *time-*"

Luke reached for the torch. "Carry me. Let's do this together. Do this for me. Please."

Evan started to speak, but paused. He took the torch from the athlete and handed it to Luke. Evan lifted Luke into his arms and carried him, moving slowly around the track, passing applauding spectators and athletes.

As they made their way up the staircase leading to the bowl for the flame, the announcer's voice blared through the speakers. "What a glorious thing to witness. It should be stated that Evan Galloway stopped at the finish line, turned around, and carried his brother to the finish line."

Evan wasn't sure how much time there was now before Dana activated the Nan Airs, but he knew that this was the right thing. Not for him, but for his brother. During the Aletheia, he had done the right thing.

Now people applauded that act. The spectators in the stadium were on their feet. The Olympians were applauding as well. Evan felt tears stinging his eyes, and didn't know whether it was because of the power of the moment, because of his dying brother in his arms, or both.

They reached the Olympic cauldron. For a moment, they paused there, the moment stretching out.

"Thank you, Evan," Luke said.

Luke lowered the torch to the cauldron, and the cone was ablaze in seconds, a roaring inferno ten feet high. The stadium erupted and Evan and Luke watched the spectacle in silence. Overhead, the sky filled with doves, flapping their wings toward the stadium's roof.

Evan looked down and saw that Luke was unconscious. He sprinted down the staircase with Luke in his arms, and was surrounded by medical people. He handed Luke to a doctor. "Get him to an MRI—"

Suddenly, the stadium's speakers crackled.

"No!" Dana's voice carried over the sound system. "This is wrong! Wrong!"

Evan knew where she had to be. He grabbed a volunteer. "Which way to your communications room?"

Forty-Five

Dana stood there, the gun shaking in front of her. Evan's "act of sportsman-ship" had been sickening, as if crossing the finish line with his brother was some kind of statement, or somehow redeemed Luke for using drugs his whole athletic career. Each flicker of the Olympic flame made her angrier. She glared at the small screen with rage, gripping the microphone in her hand tightly. "Look at yourselves," she said. "Applauding a league of cheats. Sitting in a stadium where officials and organizers don't stop the rot of corruption. Where half of them are corrupt themselves."

There were boos from the crowd. Then, hundreds of people synchronized in objection. They pointed their fingers and fists at the big screen, shouting and demanding that Dana be silent.

David was seated behind Dana. "No one's going to listen to you."

She spun around. "No, no one listens. That's the problem. The problem with people like you, David. How long have you been trying to stop those who cheat the system?"

"My whole career," David said with something close to pride.

"You strip them of their medals, ban them from playing, and yet sports remain dirty. You're worse than useless."

"And what would you do differently?" David asked.

"I'll teach them a lesson that won't be forgotten," Dana said. She had the control in her pocket. She could do it now, but people needed to understand what was happening. They needed to know *why* it was happening.

Dana raised her voice into the microphone. "Look closer at your Olympic athletes," she said. On the Operations Center's screens, the athletes were trying to figure out what was happening. The crowd had quieted. They were listening.

"You think they are so glorious, so *honorable*," Dana said. "Olympians used to compete in a spirit of chivalry, for the glory of sport. That time has passed. These athletes before you are shadows of their Olympic predecessors."

The crowd grew quieter, and surveyed the field.

"Pumping through the veins of many of these athletes is a powerful performance enhancer." She pulled the triggering device from her pocket. "They thought that they could take it without any ill effects. They thought that they wouldn't be detected or punished. They will be punished, and you will all be able to see which of them have cheated. It's time they received the punishment they deserve, a punishment that fits the crime."

Dana pressed the button on her device, expecting the athletes to clutch their chests anxiously as they felt the Nan Airs explode in their bodies, or fall to their knees in desperation.

But they didn't react. Nothing happened.

* * *

Evan approached the front door to the communications room. Tim stood with his back against the wall.

"She's in there," he said, breathing heavily.

Evan needed to know. "Did you block the signal?"

"I've lowered two layers of those thermal blankets from the roof to coat the outside of the room on every side."

"You turned the room into a faraday cage?"

"But she'll figure it out. And when she does, there won't be enough MRIs to cure all those athletes out there."

"I'm going to see if I can talk her down." Evan put a hand on Tim's shoulder. "Make sure no one gets to those blankets."

"You got it." Tim jogged down the hall, ascended pull-down stairs hanging from the ceiling and disappeared in the rafters.

Evan knocked on the door. "Dana."

There was a thud on the other side. Then silence. He heard footsteps and then his former boss' voice.

"Evan?" She laughed. "How are you, my dear?"

"After 700 miles?" Evan sighed. "Kinda beat, actually."

"I'm proud of you, really. But listen, I'm a little busy. What can I do for you?"

"I'm guessing you're having some trouble with that triggering device of yours?"

There was no response.

"Why don't you let me in? I might be able to help troubleshoot."

"And why would I do that?"

"Because I know why the signal's blocked."

Seconds passed, and then Evan heard Dana's feet shuffle. The door swung open and Evan had a pistol in his face. "Nice and slow," she said, directing Evan into the room. "Right over next to our friend David."

Evan sat down in a chair next to David Thompson. Evan remembered the man from McKnight's party. He nodded and David returned the greeting.

"What the hell are you doing, Dana?" Evan asked. "Are you out of your mind?"

Dana shrugged. "I was impressed with your performance at DARPA, you know. You were as good as MIT said you were. You figured out the Nan Airs in less than a month."

"You never wanted the Nan Airs to work. You wanted them to kill."

"The Pentagon wanted them to kill. I was just following orders."

"You should have told me and Tim that there were two *Excelsior* projects. And when Weng did figure it out, you used them for your own personal vendetta?"

"Someone had to do something. At first I just wanted to kill McKnight, but this... this is better, Evan."

David chimed in. "We could have handled this scandal, just like the others before it."

Dana scoffed. "You guys are wimps. You've let athletes walk all over you for years." She pointed to the video screen, at the athletes milling around the track. "People like you lack the courage to do what's necessary."

Evan looked over at her. "Is it wrong for those Olympians to dope? Yes, of course. But what you're doing isn't right either."

"Where the only choice is between evil and evil, I simply choose the lesser evil." She pressed the barrel of her gun against David's face. "Evan, I let you in here because you say you can help, not to debate ethics. Either you unblock the signal, or he dies."

David shook his head. "Don't do it."

"So virtuous," Dana said, "Offering to trade his life for the Olympians." She narrowed her eyes. "I *will* do it, Evan."

"I believe you," Evan said.

"How did you guys block the signal?" Dana demanded.

"Tim coated the room with a couple of layers of those thermal blankets."

Dana looked almost proud. "You made a Faraday cage?"

Evan shrugged.

"Very smart." She put the gun to David's temple. "Tell Tim to get rid of it."

"I'll need to get to the door." Evan walked over to it while Dana covered him. He shouted through it. "Tim? Tim. Lift the blankets."

"What?"

"Just do it, alright."

There was silence, followed by Tim's voice through the door. "It's done."

"Then *we're* done." Dana's revolution was underway. She pointed her gun at the nearest of the producers. "Get a camera on me." She lifted a syringe from her pocket, and presented it to the camera.

"Ladies and gentlemen, the time has come to see which of your athletes are cheating. Some of them have taken a revolutionary new drug contained in this syringe. But this drug can also be a killer. Watch closely, and you'll see who's cheating."

She lifted the triggering device, ready to make her grand statement to the world—

Suddenly, a runner sprinted across the field at a blistering speed, weaving and dodging heated fans and worried athletes. Dana leaned close to the screen, trying to identify the figure, but he was too fast, like a flash of lighting.

Evan saw this from his seat, and leaned forward with curiosity. The man looked fit, but didn't quite have the physique or the virility of an Olympian. The runner reached the end of the track, passing Theodore's chariot. He reached the bottom of the steps that led to the Olympic cauldron and paused. Then he galloped up the steps toward the fire.

Dana jammed her gun into the producer's side. "Zoom in on that man."

The producer spoke into his headset. "Camera 20: come in tight on the runner." The camera centered on him, but it only showed his back. The man stopped at the edge of the cauldron, and spun around.

It was Lucian.

David said, "Lucian Atticus?"

"Who the *hell* is that?" Dana fumed.

Evan said, "He was banned from the Olympics years ago for doping." Evan's pride was difficult to conceal. "He was my trainer."

They all turned back to the screen. Lucian pulled his jersey off and held it by his side, as he stared into the flames.

"That's an old Greek Olympic jersey," David said.

Evan recognized it from Lucian's gym.

Lucian balled up the jersey, and tossed it into the fire. The camera zoomed in on the fire, which flared up as the fabric ignited.

Then an Olympic athlete burst into a run and sprinted up the stairs next to Lucian. He, too, tore off his jersey and threw it in the flames. Another athlete did the same, then another, then more—even women stripped down to sports bras—until the stairs to the cauldron were crowded with athletes carrying their jerseys in hand, all eventually casting them into the flames.

Dana went ballistic, and screamed into the microphone. "You think you're making some kind of statement! You've made your choice!"

"It's not a choice, Dana," Evan said. "It's a distraction."

Dana spun back towards him, but Evan was already grabbing for her. He knocked the triggering device from her hand, bearing her to the ground.

In other circumstances, it wouldn't have been a fair fight, but now he was so exhausted he could barely do even that. Dana broke clear, bringing up her gun.

Bound as he was, David Thompson threw his chair forward to slam into her legs. Evan tackled her again, this time grabbing for her gun arm. A shot rang out, the bullet hitting a TV monitor behind Thompson. Evan wrestled with her for the gun, trying to pull it away, trying to get it out of her grasp.

Evan yelled, "David, destroy the device!"

David ran to the device and lifted his foot high, ready to stomp. Dana smashed her head into Evan's nose and then fired, thudding a bullet into Thompson's shoulder. She quickly spun around when...

She felt a white hot pain in her neck.

Evan sunk the syringe's needle deep into her neck, emptying a full dose of Nan Airs into her jugular. She crumpled to the ground in horror.

"How... did..." she said, disoriented. She scurried across the room, gripping her neck. Evan opened the main door and saw Tim waiting for him, along with about twenty armed security guards. Evan looked around to where silvery blankets still covered the walls. "You left them in place?"

Tim nodded.

Evan yelled to David. "Push the button!"

With one hand on his bleeding shoulder, David lowered his thumb. Dana was almost at the back door when she stopped in her tracks, feeling the Nan Airs detonate in her bloodstream. She twisted back towards Evan and saw that the thermal blankets were still lowered. There had never been any way for her to use the device. They'd tricked her. Cheated *her*.

Forty-Six

Evan was exhausted and just wanted to curl up in a ball and sleep. But he knew someone had to chase Dana, someone had to end this. She was leaving behind a trail of fluid and blood, so it wasn't difficult for him to follow her as she fled the stadium. He saw a bloody handprint on the side of a temple at the edge of Athens, and continued his pursuit.

What was left of the sinking sun cast golden beams onto Athenian buildings. Evan turned a corner and the Acropolis came into view, a complex of buildings 500 feet high, and visible from almost anywhere in the city. As the sun continued to set, the colossal stone buildings and faded statues took on a magnificent honey color.

Evan saw Dana scurry clumsily up the stairs that led to the Acropolis's entrance. The site appeared closed for the night, and the crowds had dissipated, except for a few stragglers who hung by their cars and snapped pictures of the golden sky. Evan nearly collapsed from fatigue as he ascended the stairs, pushing his hands onto his knees with each arduous step. He entered the Acropolis and followed patches of blood down the central path. He passed the Temple of Athena Nike, covered in illustrations of Athenian battles. He broke into a jog, passing propylaia and a statue of Athena.

The Parthenon rose up before him. It was a grand structure with its mighty columns, and sculptures depicting myths and legends of the Gods. He walked behind the Parthenon, and saw Dana slumped against the wall, gazing out over Athens, watching the last rays of the sun disappear. She leaned her head against a pillar and rolled her eyes toward him. She no longer seemed harsh or sinister; all the disdain and hatred had retreated from her face. She managed a halfhearted smile as Evan approached. "I don't suppose you figured out a cure for the lethal Nan Airs?"

"MRI," Evan said. "The magnet pulls the fragments from the blood."

Dana shook her head proudly. She then coughed up a gob of blood. "You know that bust of Achilles from my office?"

Evan nodded.

"After you left, I put it back together, piece by piece. It always reminded me of Michael." She reached into her pocket and pulled out the crumpled photo of her son, the same one she showed Evan on the flight to Greece. "I think about him every day."

She traced her eyes up a pillar on the Parthenon. At the top was the same drawing on the wine jar at McKnight's house at Delphi. The illustration showed Achilles thrusting his spear into the Greek queen Penthesilea. Dana looked drowsy, but she looked at Penthesilea who wasn't retreating or fighting back. Evan thought of her words at Delphi, when she told the group that just before Achilles landed his final blow, he fell in love with the queen.

"Did you love me, Evan?"

Evan bit his lip and then looked off in the distance. He had.

"I'm sorry for what I did… to you… to everyone. I wanted to teach everyone a lesson. Instead, it was you who had the lessons."

Dana could barely lift her hand, but she brought it up to Evan's fingertips. As she searched his face, Evan let her slide her hand into his.

Her breathing slowed and her head bobbed up once more, eye-level with Evan's wrist. She saw the bracelet of Achilles. "They all wanted to be remembered." Her words were slow, heavy. "But they will remember you."

Evan felt Dana's hand go limp. He didn't look down, but held his gaze on the horizon.

Forty-Seven

Evan was questioned for an hour in a conference room before the local police detectives let him leave. He went through the events in the Operations Center and the race over and over, until it felt like his mind couldn't take it anymore. Finally though, they let him go.

Evan found Tim waiting for him. His friend led him down to the stadium's small medical center. There, Luke was sitting up in bed. He looked grey, but his eyes were open, and he smiled as Evan approached.

Evan patted Luke on the chest, surprised with Luke's fast recovery. "How do you feel?"

"That MRI was no picnic… but it saved my life."

"He has been very lucky," a doctor said. "In any other stadium, there would have been no MRI, but for the Olympics…" There was a knock at the door. Lucian stepped inside. "You must be sore?"

"Just a little." Evan stepped forward and the two hugged.

"I'm guessing your boss didn't make it?"

Evan shook his head. He'd been over it too many times in the last hour. "What about McKnight?"

Evan shook his head again.

"It's as it should be."

Evan slid the bracelet of Achilles off his wrist. "I believe this belongs to you."

Lucian smiled at that. "Thank you."

He put the bracelet on his wrist.

"I couldn't have finished the race without you," Evan said.

"Nah, you could have." Lucian slapped Evan on the back. "You just would have finished in 15th place."

The group made their way into the stadium. Many of the spectators had left, but those who had stayed were walking around the field aimlessly, mixed in with the Olympic athletes.

David Thompson centered himself behind a podium on a stage. He was wearing an arm brace from the gunshot wound. "Ladies and gentlemen," he said through the stadium's sound system. "I know tonight's ceremony hasn't quite gone to plan, but I think this is as good a time as any to officially welcome you to the start of the Olympic Games."

David adjusted the microphone. "I believe that sport is a microcosm of society, and that many of the moral norms in society are reflected in athletics. With an increasingly cut-throat culture, athletes perhaps believe that only the most deceptive can win. I think we have been waiting for someone to challenge these values, to show us a new, more hopeful model of fair play. Well, we have been given that vision."

David lifted his chin proudly. "As president of the International Olympic Committee, I am afforded the right to give out certain awards to deserving athletes. Every four years, I hand out one award to someone who personifies the spirit of sportsmanship, self-sacrifice, and courage. I can't think of anyone more deserving of the Pierre de Coubertin Medal than the winner of the *Aletheia*... Evan Galloway."

The crowd erupted as Evan walked toward the stage. As he cut through the crowd, Isabella grabbed his hand. She pulled him close and kissed him. "See you after." She released him to the stage.

David placed a medal around Evan's neck. "A few words," David said, stretching his hand toward the podium.

Evan stepped forward. For a moment, he just gazed into the sea of people. "Thank you, David, for this award—it's truly an honor."

He looked pensive. "I think it's natural for athletes to want to test our limits. As technology continues to advance, we will constantly be tempted to seek out enhancements—new technologies that will no doubt outpace our understanding of the ethical consequences. If I have learned anything in the past year, it's that we don't need artificial aid to test our limits. We can do that on our own. Thank you again, David, for this great honor, and I wish you all the best of luck in these Games."

Evan waved a few times and then stepped off the stage and made his way through the crowd. Luke followed Evan as he walked. "So what're you going to do now?"

"I'm going to sleep for a week," Evan said. "Then I'm going to call General Somervell, tell him the real story behind the *Excelsior* program. After that, I don't know. Maybe I'll see if there's a faculty position open at MIT. Or maybe I'll start my own lab. Who knows, Coach Helmsley's always looking for help."

By the time Evan had reached Lucian, the old man was sitting on the track, lacing up his running shoes. Isabella appeared by Evan's side. "Let's all go for a drink."

"What do you say, Lucian?" Evan asked.

Lucian tied the last knot on his shoelace. He reached into his duffel bag, and Evan knew he was going for a flask. But Lucian pulled out a bottle of olive oil and handed it to Evan with a grin. "I'm going for a jog." He looked down the running track.

Evan turned the bottle over in his hands. "A superior product?"

"A superior man," Lucian said. He then burst into a sprint down the Olympic track.

THE END

Made in the USA
Columbia, SC
10 June 2018